INTER... GROOMS

Choose your dream destination to say "I Do"!

Applegate Ranch, Montana:
Get your lasso at the ready for rugged rancher Dillon in
RODEO BRIDE by Myrna Mackenzie

Loire Valley, France:
You don't need a magic wand for a fairy tale in France,
with handsome château owner Alex as your host!
CINDERELLA ON HIS DOORSTEP
by Rebecca Winters

Principality of Carvainia, Mediterranean:
Step into Aleks's turreted castle
and you'll feel like a princess!
HER PRINCE'S SECRET SON
by Linda Goodnight

Manhattan, New York:
Stroll down Fifth Avenue
on the arm of self-made millionaire Houston.
RESCUED IN A WEDDING DRESS
by Cara Colter

Naples, Italy:
The majesty of Mount Vesuvius and dangerously
dashing Dante will make your senses erupt!
ACCIDENTALLY EXPECTING!
by Lucy Gordon

Sydney, Australia:
Hotshot TV producer Dan is on the lookout
for someone to star in his life....
LIGHTS, CAMERA...KISS THE BOSS
by Nikki Logan

Alex tilted his dark head. "By sunset Rapunzel will be safely ensconced in her tower."

Dana chuckled to hide her excitement at spending the day with him, not to mention the rest of the month. "You're mixing up your fairy tales. I don't have long hair."

He gave an elegant shrug of his broad shoulders. "Her father had her long golden tresses cut off so no prince could climb up to her."

Dana stopped dead in her tracks. In the tale she'd grown up with there'd been a wicked witch. Was he still teasing her, or had this tale suddenly taken on a life of its own? "Then how did the prince reach her?"

He paused in the doorway. "I guess you'll have to read the end of the story to find out."

REBECCA WINTERS

Cinderella on His Doorstep

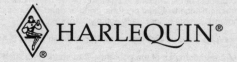

TORONTO • NEW YORK • LONDON
AMSTERDAM • PARIS • SYDNEY • HAMBURG
STOCKHOLM • ATHENS • TOKYO • MILAN • MADRID
PRAGUE • WARSAW • BUDAPEST • AUCKLAND

Recycling programs
for this product may
not exist in your area.

ISBN-13: 978-0-373-74007-9

CINDERELLA ON HIS DOORSTEP

First North American Publication 2010.

Printed in U.S.A.

This is Rebecca Winters's 100th book!

Rebecca has taken readers on many wonderful journeys, and this story is no exception. She'll capture your soul with the smells, sounds and flavors of France…and steal your heart with a romance to treasure!

Praise for some of Rebecca's stories

"Rebecca Winters…is a page-turner.
The hero and heroine really shine,
with delightful scenes and great dialogue."
—*RT Book Reviews*

"A very intense, emotional story that unfolds a charming romance and endearing characters."
—*RT Book Reviews*

**Rebecca loves to hear from her readers.
If you wish to e-mail her, please visit her
Web site at www.cleanromances.com.**

To my son, Bill,
whom I often call Guillaume because he speaks
French, too, and loved France and the vineyards
as much as I did when we traveled there. I called
upon him for some of the research for this book.
Once again we had a marvelous time discussing
one of France's greatest contributions to the world.

A special bonus from Rebecca…
Ten Things I Love About France

1. The French language itself. Can you imagine anything more delightful than the name *Marguerite* for a daisy? They grow wild around the châteaux.

2. The Château de Chenonceau in the Loire Valley. It stretches on white stone piers across the river whose grounds are adorned with rose gardens and mazes, a place to capture a young woman's heart.

3. Lines of green vineyards along the 650-mile course of the Loire where kings built their residences. Chenin Blanc grapes that make sweet white dessert wine.

4. The marvelous fresh scent of lavender fields.

5. Golden wheat and sunflowers.

6. Paintings of Monet, van Gogh, Renoir.

7. Pont-Évêque and Maroilles cheeses.

8. The lazy Layon, a tributary of the Loire, overgrown with greenery the French Impressionists captured in their masterpieces.

9. The pottery of La Borne's tiny village nestled in the Loire Valley.

10. Last, but not least, French bread! The baguette.

CHAPTER ONE

Sanur, Bali—June 2

"MARTAN?"

Through the shower of a light rain Alex Martin heard his name being called from clear down the street. He paused in the front doorway with his suitcases. The houseboy whose now-deceased mother had been hired by the Forsten Project years earlier to help clean the employees' houses, had attached himself to Alex. Without fail, he always called him by his last name, giving it a French pronunciation.

"Hey, Sapto—I didn't think I was going to see you again." He'd been waiting for the taxi that would drive him to the Sanur airport in Bali.

Before the accident that had killed William Martin, Alex's Australian-born father, William would turn on Sapto. "Our last name is *Martin*! Mar-TIN!"

Sapto had stubbornly refused to comply. In recent months he'd lost his mother in a flood and knew Alex had lost his French mother to an aggressive infection several years back. He felt they had a bond. Alex had been rather touched by the boy's sensitivity and never tried to correct him.

"Take me home with you." His dark eyes begged him. "I've never been to France."

Home? That was a strange thing for Sapto to say. Though Alex held dual citizenship and was bilingual, he'd never been to France, either. As for Sapto, he guessed the fifteen-year-old hadn't ventured farther than twenty miles from Sanur in the whole of his life.

Alex's family had moved wherever his father's work as a mechanical engineer had taken him, first in Australia, then Africa and eventually Indonesia. With his parents gone, he didn't consider anywhere home. After flying to Australia to bury his father next to his mother, he was aware of an emptiness that prevented him from feeling an emotional tie to any given spot.

"I wish I could, Sapto, but I don't know what my future's going to be from here on out."

"But you said your French grandfather left you a house when he died! I could live there and clean it for you."

Alex grimaced. "He didn't leave it to *me*, Sapto." The letter meant for his mother had come two years too late. It had finally caught up to Alex through the Forsten company where he worked.

The attorney who'd written it stated there was going to be a probate hearing for the Fleury property on June 5 in Angers, France. This was the last notice. If Genevieve Fleury, the only living member of the Fleury family didn't appear for it, the property located in the Loire Valley would be turned over to the French government.

After making a phone call to the attorney and identifying himself, Alex was told the estate had been neglected for forty odd years and had dwindled into an old relic beyond salvaging. The back taxes owing were prohibitive.

Be that as it may, Alex had the impression the attorney was downplaying its value for a reason. A piece of ground was always worth something. In fact, the other man hadn't been able to cover his shock when he'd learned it was Genevieve's son on the phone.

Something wasn't right.

At this point the one thing driving Alex was the need to visit the land of his mother's roots and get to the bottom of this mystery before moving on. With no family ties, he was free to set up his own company in the States.

By now the taxi had arrived. Sapto put his bags in the trunk for him. "You will write me, yes?" His eyes glistened with tears.

"I promise to send you a postcard." He slipped a cash bonus into the teen's hand. "Thank you for all your help. I won't forget. Take care."

"Goodbye," Sapto called back, running after the taxi until it rounded the corner.

Hollywood, California—August 2

"Lunch break! Meet back here at one o'clock. No excuses!"

With the strongly accented edict that had been awaited for over an hour, the actors and cameramen left the set in a stampede.

When Jan Lofgren's thick brows met together, Dana knew her genius father was in one of his moods. Most of the time the Swedish-born director was so caught up in the story he wanted to bring to life, he lived in another realm and lost patience with human weaknesses and imperfections of any kind, especially hers.

As his only offspring, she'd been a big disappointment. He'd wanted a brilliant son. Instead he got a mediocre daughter, whose average brain and looks would never make her fortune. When she was a little girl her mother had cautioned her, "Your father loves you, honey, but don't expect him to be like anyone else. With that ego of his, he's a difficult man to love. You have to take him the way he is, or suffer."

The truth was as hard to take today as it was then. Dana had been through a lot of grief since her mother's death five years ago, but had learned to keep it to herself. Especially lately while he was having problems with his present girlfriend, Saskia Brusse, a Dutch model turned aspiring actress who had a bit part in this film. She wasn't much older than Dana's twenty-six years, the antithesis of Dana's mother in every conceivable way.

Privately his love life pained and embarrassed Dana, but she would never have dared articulate her disapproval. The same couldn't be said of her father who'd been outspoken about her disastrous relationship with Neal Robeson, a young actor looking for an in with the famous director, rather than with her. She'd thought she'd found love. Her mistake. It was a lesson in humiliation she would never forget.

Granted she'd made a gross error in getting

involved with anyone in the film industry, but for her father to explode over that when he never seemed to notice anything else she did for him had caused a serious rift between them. It would never heal if left up to him, not when his anger was over the top. Once again she found herself making overtures to breach the gap.

"I brought you some coffee and sandwiches."

Deep in thought he took the thermos from her and began drinking the hot liquid. After another long swallow he said, "I've decided to shoot the rest of this film on location. Then it will ripen into something worthy."

Her father needed atmosphere, that ethereal ingredient the studio set couldn't provide. He flicked her a speculative glance. "Everything's in place except for the most important segment of the film in France. I'm not happy with any of our old options and want something different."

Dana already knew that and was ready for him. Since her mother's funeral, finding the right locations had become Dana's main job besides being chief cook and general dogsbody to her irascible father. She had to concede he paid her well, but the sense that she was invisible to him inflicted a deep wound.

If he wasn't directing one of his award-winning films, he had his nose in a biography. She was a voracious reader, too, and had inherited his love of firsthand accounts of World War II in the European theatre. Over the years they'd traipsed from the coast of England to the continent, pinpointing the exact locales to bring his creations to life.

"I've come across something on the Internet that sounds promising, but I'll need to check it out first. Give me a couple of days." If she could solve this problem for him, maybe he'd remember he had a daughter who yearned for a little attention from him. When she was his own flesh and blood, it hurt to be a mere cipher.

"That's too long."

"I can only get to Paris in so many hours, but once I'm there, I'll make up for lost time. Expect to hear from me tomorrow evening."

"What's your final destination?"

"I'd rather not say." She could hope that if she found what he was looking for, it would ease some of the tension between them, but she doubted it because her mother had been the only one who knew how to soothe him. Now that she was gone, no one seemed to exist for him, especially not his only child.

* * *

Around the next bend of the Layon river, Dana crossed a stone bridge where she saw the sign for Rablay-sur-Layon. So much greenery made her feel as if she'd driven into a Monet painting done at Giverny and had become a part of it. The string of Anjou region villages nestled against this tributary of the Loire gave off an aura of timeless enchantment.

How shocking it must have been for the French people to see soldiers and tanks silhouetted against gentle slopes of sunflowers as they gouged their way through this peaceful, fertile river valley. Dana cringed to imagine the desecration of a landscape dotted with renaissance chateaux and vineyards of incomparable beauty.

A loud hunger pain resounded in the rental car. Between her empty stomach and the long shadows cast by a setting sun, it occurred to her she ought to have eaten dinner at the last village she'd passed and waited till morning to reach her destination. However, she wasn't her father's daughter for nothing and tended to ignore sensible restrictions in order to gratify certain impulses for which she often paid a price.

No matter. She wanted to see how the light played against the Château de Belles Fleurs as it faded into darkness. One look and she'd be able to tell if this place had that unique ambience her father demanded.

Following the map she'd printed off, Dana made a right at the second turn from the bridge and passed through an open grillwork gate. From there she proceeded to the bifurcation where she took the right fork. Suddenly she came upon the estate, but unlike the carefully groomed grounds of any number of chateaux she'd glimpsed en route, this was so overgrown she was put in mind of a *bois sauvage*. Without directions she would never have known of its existence, let alone stumbled on to it by accident.

A little farther now and a *tour* of the chateau's bastion with its pointed cone appeared as if it were playing hide-and-seek behind the heavy foliage. Clumps of plum-colored wild roses had run rampant throughout, merging with a tall hedge that had long since grown wild and lost its shape.

She pulled to a stop and got out of the car, compelled to explore this ungovernable wood filled with wild daisies hidden in clumps of brush. Once she'd penetrated deeper on foot, she peeked through the tree leaves, but was unable to glimpse more.

A lonely feeling stole through her. No one

had lived here for years. The estate had an untouched quality. Secrets. She knew in her bones these intangible elements would appeal to her father. If she'd combed the entire Loire valley, she couldn't have found a more perfect spot. He demanded perfection.

"Puis-je vous aider, madame?" came the sound of a deep male voice.

Startled out of her wits, Dana spun around. "Oh—" she cried at the sight of the bronzed, dark-haired man who looked to be in his midthirties. "I didn't know anyone was here." Her tourist French was of no help in this situation, but judging by his next remark, she needn't have worried.

"Nor did I." His English sounded as authentic as his French, but she couldn't place the pronunciation. His tone came off borderline aggressive.

His hands were thrust in the back pockets of well-worn, thigh-molding jeans. With those long, powerful legs and cut physique visible beneath a soil-stained white T-shirt, she estimated he was six-three and spent most of his time in the sun.

"The place looks deserted. Are you the caretaker here?"

He flashed her a faintly mocking smile. "In a

manner of speaking. Are you lost?" She had the impression he was impatient to get on with what he'd been doing before she'd trespassed unannounced. Twilight was deepening into night, obscuring the details of his striking features.

"No. I planned to come here in the morning, but my curiosity wouldn't let me wait that long to get a sneak preview."

His dark-fringed eyes studied her with toe-curling intensity. For once she wished she were a tall, lovely brunette like her mom instead of your average Swedish blonde with generic blue eyes, her legacy from the Lofgren gene pool.

"If you're a Realtor for an American client, I'm afraid the property isn't for sale."

She frowned. "I'm here for a different reason. This *is* the Château de Belles Fleurs, isn't it?"

He gave an almost imperceptible nod, drawing her attention to his head of overly long dark hair with just enough curl she wagered her balding father would kill for.

"I'm anxious to meet the present owner, Monsieur Alexandre Fleury Martin."

After an odd silence he said, "You're speaking to him."

"Oh—I'm sorry. I didn't realize."

He folded his strong arms, making her

acutely aware of his stunning male aura. "How do you know my name?"

"I came across a French link to your advertisement on the Internet."

At her explanation his hard-muscled body seemed to tauten. "Unfortunately too many tourists have seen it and decided to include a drop-in visit on their 'see-France-in-seven-days' itinerary."

Uh-oh— Her uninvited presence had touched a nerve. She lifted her oval chin a trifle. "Perhaps you should get a guard dog, or lock the outer gate with a sign that says, No Trespassing."

"Believe me, I'm considering both."

She bit her lip. "Look—this has started off all wrong and it's my fault." When he didn't respond she said, "My name is Dana Lofgren. If you're a movie buff, you may have seen *The Belgian Connection*, one of the films my father directed."

He rubbed his chest without seeming to be conscious of it. "I didn't know Jan Lofgren had a daughter."

Most people didn't except for those in the industry who worked with her father. Of course if Dana had been born with a face and body to die for…

She smiled, long since resigned to being for-gettable. "Why would you? I help my father behind the scenes. The moment I saw your ad, I flew from Los Angeles to check out your estate. He's working on the film right now, but isn't happy with the French locations available."

Dana heard him take a deep breath. "You should have e-mailed me you were coming so I could have met you in Angers. It's too late to see anything tonight."

"I didn't expect to meet you until tomorrow," she said, aware she'd angered him without meaning to. "Forgive me for scouting around without your permission. I wanted to get a feel for the place in the fading light."

"And did you?" he fired. It was no idle question.

"Yes."

The silly tremor in her voice must have conveyed her emotion over the find because he said, "We'll talk about it over dinner. I haven't had mine yet. Where are you staying tonight?"

Considering her major faux pas for intruding on his privacy, she was surprised there was going to be one. "I made a reservation at the Hermitage in Chanzeaux."

"Good. That's not far from here. I'll change

my clothes and follow you there in my car. Wait for me in yours and lock the doors."

The enigmatic owner accompanied her to the rental car. As he opened the door for her, their arms brushed, sending a surprising curl of warmth through her body.

"I won't be long."

She watched his tall, well-honed physique disappear around the end of the hedge. Obviously there was a path, but she hadn't noticed. There'd been too much to take in.

Now an unexpected human element had been added. It troubled her that she was still reacting to the contact. She thought she'd already learned her lesson about men.

Alex signaled the waiter. "Bring us your best house wine, *s'il vous plait.*"

"*Oui, monsieur.*"

When he'd come up with his idea to rent out the estate to film studios in order to make a lot of money fast, he hadn't expected a Hollywood company featuring a legendary director like Jan Lofgren to take an interest this soon, if ever.

He'd only been advertising the château for six weeks. Not every film company wanted a place this run-down. To make it habitable, he'd had new tubs, showers, toilets and sinks installed in both the bathroom off the second floor vestibule and behind the kitchen.

Alex needed close access to the outside for himself and any workmen he hired, not to mention the film crews and actors. The ancient plumbing in both bathrooms had to be pulled out. He'd spent several days replacing corroded pipes with new ones that met modern code.

Since then, three different studios from Paris had already done some sequence shots along the river using the château in the background, but they were on limited budgets.

It would take several years of that kind of continual traffic to fatten his bank account to the amount he needed. By then the deadline for the taxes owing would have passed and he would forfeit the estate.

So far, at least fifty would-be investors ranging from locals to foreigners were dying to get their hands on it so they could turn it into a hotel. One of them included the attorney who'd sent out the letter, but Alex had no intention of letting his mother's inheritance go if he could help it.

With the natural blonde beauty seated across from him, it was possible he could shorten the time span for that happening. There was hope yet. She hadn't been turned off by what she'd seen or she wouldn't be eating dinner with him now. Her father was a huge moneymaker for the producers. His films guaranteed a big budget. Alex was prepared to go out on a limb for her.

Dana Lofgren didn't look older than twenty-two, twenty-three, yet age could be deceptive. She might be young, but being the director's only child she'd grown up with him and knew him as no one else did or could. If she thought the estate had promise, her opinion would carry a lot of weight with him. Hopefully word of mouth would spread to other studios.

After spending all day every day clearing away tons of brush and debris built up around the château over four decades, her unexplained presence no matter how feminine or attractive, hadn't helped his foul mood. That was before he realized she had a legitimate reason for looking around, even if she'd wandered in uninvited.

"How did you like your food?"

She lifted flame-blue eyes to him. With all that silky gold hair and a cupid mouth, she reminded him of a cherub, albeit a grown-up one radiating a sensuality of which she seemed totally unaware. "The chateaubriand was delicious."

"That's good. I've sampled all their entrées

and can assure you the meals here will keep any film crew happy."

His dinner companion wiped the corner of her mouth with her napkin. "I can believe it. One could put on a lot of weight staying here for any length of time. It's a good thing I'm not a film star."

An underweight actress might look good in front of the camera, but Alex preferred a woman who looked healthy, like this one whose cheeks glowed a soft pink in the candlelight.

"No ambition in that department?"

"None."

He believed her. "What *are* you, when you're not helping your father?"

The bleak expression in her eyes didn't match her low chuckle. "That's a good question."

"Let me rephrase it. What is it you do in your spare time?"

The waiter brought their crème brûlée to the table. She waited until he'd poured them more wine before answering Alex. "Nothing of report. I read and play around with cooking. Otherwise my father forgets to eat."

"You live with him?"

Instead of answering him, she sipped the wine experimentally. Mmm...it was so sweet.

She took a bite of custard from the ramekin, then drank more. He could tell she loved it. "This could become addicting."

Alex enjoyed watching her savor her meal. "If I seemed to get too personal just now, it's because the widowed grandfather I never knew threw my mother out of the château when she was about your age. Both of them died without ever seeing each other again."

Her ringless fingers tightened around the stem of her wineglass. "Since my mother died of cancer five years ago, my father and I have gone the rounds many times, but it hasn't come to that yet." She took another sip. "The fact is, whether we're at home or on location, which is most of the time, he needs a keeper."

Amused by her last comment he said, "It's nice to hear of a father-daughter relationship that works. You're both fortunate."

A subtle change fell over her. "Your mother's story is very tragic. If you don't mind my asking, what caused such a terrible breach?"

Maybe it was his imagination but she sounded sincere in wanting to know.

"Gaston Fleury lost his only son in war, causing both my grandparents to wallow in grief. When my grandmother died, he gave up living, even though he had a daughter who would have done anything for him. The more she tried to love him, the colder he became.

"Obviously he'd experienced some kind of mental breakdown because he turned inward, unable to love anyone. He forgot his daughter existed and became a total recluse, letting everything go including his household staff. When my mother tried to work with him, he told her to get out. He didn't need anyone."

In the telling, his dinner companion's eyes developed a fine sheen. What was going on inside her?

"Horrified by the change in him, she made the decision to marry my father, who'd come to France on vacation. They moved to Queensland, Australia, where he was born."

"Is your father still there?"

"No. He died in a fatal car accident seven months ago."

She stirred restlessly. "You've been through a lot of grief."

"It's life, as you've found out."

"Yes," she murmured.

"My father's animosity toward my grandfather was so great, he didn't tell me the whole story until after mother died of an infection two years ago. Gaston never wrote or sent for her, so she never went back for a visit, not even after I was born. The pain would have been too great. It explained her lifelong sadness."

Earnest eyes searched his. "Growing up you must have wondered," she whispered.

He nodded. "To make a long story short, in May a letter meant for Mother fell into my hands. The attorney for the abandoned Belles Fleurs estate had been trying to find her. When I spoke with him personally he told me my grandfather had died in a government institution and was buried in an unmarked grave."

She shook her head. "That's awful."

"Agreed. If she didn't fly to France for a probate hearing, the property would be turned over to the government for years of back taxes owing. It consisted of a neglected château and grounds. I discovered very quickly the whole estate is half buried in vegetation like one of those Mayan temples in Central America."

The corners of her mouth lifted. "A perfect simile."

"However, something inside me couldn't let it go without a fight. That meant I needed to make money in a hurry. So I came up with the idea of renting out the property to film studios."

She eyed him frankly. "That was a brilliant move on your part for which my father will be ecstatic. You're a very resourceful man. I hope your ad continues to bring you all the business you need in order to hold on to it."

Dana Lofgren was a refreshing change from most women of his acquaintance who came on to him without provocation. While they'd eaten a meal together, she'd listened to him without giving away much about herself.

Alex couldn't tell if it was a defense mechanism or simply the way she'd been born, but the fact remained she'd come as a pleasant surprise on many levels. He found he didn't want the evening to end, but sensed she was ready to say good-night.

When he'd finished his wine, he put some bills on the table. "After your long flight and the drive from Paris, you have to be exhausted. What time would you like to come to the château tomorrow?"

"Early, if that's all right with you. Maybe 8:00 a.m.?"

An early bird. Alex liked doing business early. *"Bon."* He pushed himself away from the table and stood up. "I'll be waiting for you in the drive. *Bonuit, mademoiselle.*"

* * *

Monsieur Martin not only intrigued Dana, but he'd left her with a lot to think about. In fact, the tragedy he'd related had shaken her. His mother had become invisible to her own father, too. There were too many similarities to Dana's life she didn't want to contemplate.

She finished the last of her wine, upset with herself for letting Monsieur Martin's male charisma prompt her to get more personal with him and prod him for details about his family. That was how she'd gotten into trouble with Neal. He'd pretended to be flattered by all her interest. She'd thought they were headed toward something permanent until she realized it was her father who'd brought him around in the first place—that, and his ambition.

Of course there was a big difference here. Neal had used her in the hope of acting in one of her father's films. She on the other hand had flown to France because Monsieur Martin had advertised his property for a specific clientele. Dana wanted a service from *him*. The two situations weren't comparable.

Neither were the two men....

At her first sight of the striking owner, Dana was convinced she'd come upon the château of the sleeping prince, and *that* before the wine had put her in such a mellow mood. But their subsequent conversation soon jerked her out of that fantasy.

He was a tough, intelligent businessman of substance with an aura of authority she would imagine intimidated most men. Maybe even her own scary parent. That would be something to witness.

Disciplining herself not to eat the last few bites of custard, she left the dining room and went to her room. She could phone her father tonight with the good news. He'd be awake by now expecting her call, unless he'd spent the night with Saskia, which was a strong possibility.

All things considered, she decided to get in touch with him tomorrow after she'd met with Monsieur Martin again.

After getting ready for bed, she set her alarm for 7:00 a.m. She was afraid she'd sleep in otherwise, but to her surprise, Dana awoke before it went off because she was too excited for the day.

She took a shower and washed her hair. Her neck-length layered cut fell into place fast using her blow-dryer. Afterward she put on her favorite Italian blouse. It was a dark blue cotton jersey with a high neck and three-quarter sleeves, casual yet professional.

She teamed it with beige voile pants and Italian bone-colored sandals. Since she was only five foot five, she hoped the straight-leg style gave the illusion of another inch of height. Dana was built curvy like her mother. Being around Monsieur Martin, she could have wished for a few more inches from her father who stood six-one. Barring that, all she could do was keep a straight carriage.

With her bag packed, she headed for the dining room where rolls and coffee were being served. She grabbed a quick breakfast, then walked out to talk to a woman at the front desk Dana hadn't seen yesterday. "*Bonjour*, madame."

"*Bonjour, madame*. How can I help you?"

"I'm checking out." After she'd handed her back the credit card, Dana said, "Last night I drank a wonderful white wine in the restaurant and would like to buy a bottle to take home with me." Her father would love it. "Could you tell me the name of it?"

"*Bien sur*. We only stock one kind. It's the Domaine Coteaux du Layon Percher made right here in the Anjou."

"It's one of the best wines I ever tasted."

"In my opinion, Percher is better than the other brands from this area. Sadly the most celebrated of them was the Domaine Belles Fleurs, but it stopped being produced eighty years ago."

Dana's body quickened. The woman did say Belles Fleurs. "Do you know why?"

She leaned closer. "Bad family blood." Dana had gathered as much already. There'd been a complete break between Monsieur Martin's mother and her father, but he hadn't mentioned anything else. "It's an ugly business fighting over who had the rights to what."

"I agree."

"The present owner has only lived in the vicinity a month or so," the woman confided. "The château has been deserted for many years."

So Monsieur Martin had told her. "It's very sad."

"*C'est la vie, madame,*" she said with typical Gallic fatalism. "Would you like to buy a bottle of the Percher?"

"I—I've changed my mind," her voice faltered. It would seem a betrayal.

"Is there anything else I can do for you?"

"No, *merci.*"

Dana turned away and left the hotel. She was

in a much more subdued frame of mind as she drove the five or so kilometers to the bridge where the trees cast more shadows across the road. The morning light coming from the opposite side of a pale blue sky created a totally different atmosphere from the night before.

This time as she reached the fork in the road, Monsieur Martin was there to greet her. It sent her pulse racing without her permission. She pulled to a stop.

He walked toward her, dressed in white cargo pants and a burgundy colored crewneck, but it didn't matter what he wore, she found him incredibly appealing. It wasn't just the attractive arrangement of his hard-boned features, or midnight-brown eyes framed by dark brows.

The man had an air of brooding detachment that added to her fascination. Combined with his sophistication, she imagined most women meeting him would have fantasies about him.

Under the influence of the wine, Dana had already entertained a few of her own last night. However, because of her experience with Neal, plus the fact that she was clearheaded this morning, she was determined to conduct business without being distracted.

"*Bonjour*, Monsieur Martin."

When he put his tanned hands on the door frame, the scent of the soap he'd used in the shower infiltrated below her radar. "My name's Alex. You don't mind if I call you Dana?" His voice sounded lower this morning, adding to his male sensuality.

"I'd prefer it."

"Bien." He walked around to the passenger side of her car and adjusted the seat to accommodate his long legs before climbing in. His proximity trapped the air in her lungs. "Take the left fork. It will wind around to the front of the château."

Old leaves built up over time covered the winding driveway. It was flanked on both sides by trees whose unruly tops met overhead like a Gothic arch. Dana followed until it led to a clearing where she got her first look at the small eighteenth-century château built in the classic French style.

Beyond the far end stood an outbuilding made of the same limestone and built in the same design, half camouflaged by more overgrown shrubs and foliage. No doubt it housed the winepress and vats.

She shut off the engine and climbed out to feast her eyes. He followed at a slower pace.

The signs of age and neglect showed up in full force. There were boards covering the grouped stacks of broken windows. Several steps leading to the elegant entry were chipped or cracked. Repairs needed to be done to the high-sloped slate roof. It was difficult to tell where the weed-filled gardens filled with tiny yellow lilies ended and the woods encroached.

Dana took it all in, seeing it through her father's eyes. She knew what the original script called for. This was so perfect she thought she must be dreaming.

"It's like seeing a woman of the night on the following morning when her charms are no longer in evidence," came his grating voice. Trust a man to come up with that analogy. "Not what you had in mind after all?"

Schooling herself not to react to his cynicism, she turned to her host, having sensed a certain tension emanating from him. "On the contrary. It will do better than you can imagine. Knowing how my father works, he'll need three weeks here. How soon can you give the studio that much time?"

CHAPTER TWO

FEW things had surprised Alex in life, but twice in the last eighteen hours Dana Lofgren had taken him unawares.

"I have nothing signed and sealed yet. Is the season of vital importance?"

Her nod caused her hair to gleam in the sun like fine gold mesh. "It has to be late summer. Right now if possible," she said, looking all around, "but maybe that's asking too much."

"Don't worry. It's available. My next tentative booking so far is with a Paris studio that won't be needing it until mid-September."

"Good," she murmured, almost as if she'd forgotten he was there.

"Are you ready to see the interior?"

"No." She sounded far away. "I'll leave that to my father. I've seen what's important to him. The estate possesses that intangible atmosphere he's striving for. I knew it as I drove in last night.

"Over the years of watching him work I've learned he doesn't like too much information. If I were to paint pictures, he'd see them in his mind. They would interfere with his own creative process." She suddenly turned and flashed him a quick smile. "His words, not mine."

Alex couldn't help smiling back. She had to be made of strong stuff to handle her father whose ego was probably bigger than his reputation. "Such trust in you implies a spiritual connection I think."

"I would say it has more to do with our mutual love of history. When I leave, I'll phone him and let him know what I've found. Before the day is out you'll hear from two people."

This fast she'd made her decision? Alex couldn't remember meeting anyone like her before. Did she always function on impulse, or just where her father was concerned? "I'll be waiting."

"Sol Arnevitz handles the financial arrangements. Paul Soleri is in charge of everything and everyone else when we're on location. Paul will go over the logistics and has the ability to smooth out any problem. You'll like *him*."

"As opposed to…"

She made a face. "Who else?"

Meaning her father of course. Dana Lofgren was a woman who didn't take herself too seriously. Despite what he assumed was a ten-year age difference between them, he feared she was growing on him at a time when he couldn't afford distractions.

"What more can I do for you this morning?"

"Not another thing." But her blue eyes burned with questions she didn't articulate, piquing his interest. "Thank you for dinner last night and your time this morning. It's been a real pleasure, Alex. Expect to hear from Sol right away. Here's his business card." She handed it to him. "He'll work out all the details with you."

To his shock she got in her car before he could help her.

"Where are you going in such a hurry?" He wasn't ready to let her go yet.

"A daughter's work is never done. I have to be in Paris this afternoon, then I'll fly back to L.A. Enjoy your solitude before everyone descends on you."

The next thing he knew she'd turned around and had driven off, leaving him strangely bereft and more curious than ever about her association with a father who was bigger than life in her eyes. Alex saw the signs. Ten, twenty, even thirty years from now he had a hunch Jan Lofgren's hold on her would still be powerful.

He stared blindly into space. Whether strongly present in Dana's life, or deliberately absent as Gaston Fluery had been in his daughter's life, both fathers wielded an enormous impact. The thought disturbed Alex in ways he'd rather not examine.

An hour later, after he'd changed clothes and had begun cutting down more overgrowth, his cell phone rang. It could be anyone, but in case it was Dana, he pulled it out of his pants pocket. The ID indicated a call from the States. He clicked on. "Alex Martin speaking."

"Mr. Martin? This is Pyramid Pictures Film Studio calling from Hollywood, California. If it's convenient Mr. Sol Arnevitz would like to set up a conference call with you and Mr. Paul Soleri before he goes to bed at eleven this evening. It's 7:00 p.m. now. Mr. Lofgren heard from his daughter and is anxious to move on this."

Alex was anxious, too, for several reasons. "Eight o'clock your time would work for me."

"Very good. Expect their call then."

After twenty more minutes loading the truck, Alex went back to the château and entered through a side door leading into the kitchen. He washed his hands, then poured himself a cup of coffee before carrying it to the ornate salon off the foyer, which he'd turned into a temporary bedroom-cum-office. He liked living with the few furnishings of his parents he'd had shipped.

The salon's original furniture was still stored on the top floor. Once he'd made inroads on the outside of the château, he would concentrate on the house itself, that is if he made enough money in time. For now he'd supplied himself with the necessities for living here: electricity, cable and Internet, running water hot and cold, a new water heater, a stove, a fridge, washer and dryer and a new bed with a king-size mattress and box springs.

He snagged the swivel chair with his foot and sat down at his desk. No sooner had he booted up his computer than his call came through. Once the other two men introduced themselves, they made short work of the negotiations. The company would be on location from August 8 through 31. Sol quoted a ballpark figure, but left it open because other expenses always accrued.

Alex didn't know if Dana had anything to do with the actual amount, but it was a far greater sum than he'd hoped for. Sol sent him a fax, making the contract official before he rang off.

Paul stayed on the line with him for another twenty minutes. They discussed logistics for the cameramen and staff. Alex e-mailed him a list of hotels, car rental agencies and other businesses in and around Angers such as Chanzeaux.

"Chanzeaux?" the other man said. "Dana mentioned she stayed at a hotel there last night. I believe it was the Hermitage. According to her it's the perfect place for her father."

It pleased Alex she'd given her seal of approval. "The food's exceptionally good there. Mr. Lofgren should be very comfortable."

"Since we're behind schedule as it is, we all want that," he admitted with a dry laugh that spoke volumes about Dana's father. "The crew will arrive day after tomorrow. Everyone else the day after. I look forward to meeting you, Alex."

"The feeling's mutual."

After clicking off, he headed outside again. Dana would be back in a few days, this time with her father. Over the years Alex had been involved in various relationships with women, but he'd never found himself thinking ahead to the next meeting with this kind of anticipation. He had no answer as to why this phenomenon was suddenly happening now.

* * *

During the taxi ride to the house, Dana phoned Sol whose secretary told him the contract with Mr. Martin had been signed. Relieved on that score she called Paul, wanting to touch base with him before she saw her father.

"Hey, Dana— Are you back already?"

"Yes, but only long enough to pack before I leave again. Sol says everything's ready to go."

"That's right. I've got us booked at three hotels fairly close together. Just so you know, the Hermitage didn't have any vacancies, but with a little monetary incentive I managed to arrange adjoining rooms for you and your father for the month."

She smiled. "You're indispensable, Paul."

"Tell your father that."

"I don't need to." Except that nobody told Jan Lofgren anything. Little did Paul know that even though he'd arranged a hotel room somewhere else for Saskia, she'd probably end up staying with Dana's father. "Listen, Paul—I'm almost at the house so I've got to go. Talk to you later."

"*Ciao*, Dana."

After she hung up, her mind focused on her own sleeping arrangements. Since the film studio had the run of the estate until the end of August, Dana decided she would stay in the deserted château away from everyone. When else in her life would she get a chance like this? She'd buy a sleeping bag. It would be a lark to camp out inside.

Her dad wouldn't need her except to do the odd job for him and bring him lunch. Once he settled in for work each day, he hated having to leave with the others to go eat. Maybe he used it as an excuse to be alone with his own thoughts for an hour. Who knew?

What mattered was that she'd have most of her time free to explore the countryside and only come back at dark to go to sleep. Her thoughts wandered to Alex. She wondered where he was staying. The concierge at the Hermitage indicated he lived in the vicinity. Considering the taxes he owed, she imagined he'd found a one-star hotel in order to keep his expenses down. It made her happy that the film company would be giving him a financial boost. He—

"Miss?"

Dana blinked. "Oh—yes! I'm sorry." They'd reached her family's modern rancho-styled home in Hollywood Hills without her being aware he'd stopped the taxi. She paid him and got out.

Just in case her father had brought Saskia home, she rang the doorbell several times before letting herself in. After ascertaining she was alone, Dana took off her shoes and padded into the kitchen to sort through the mail and fix some lunch.

The clock in the hall chimed once, reminding her France was nine hours ahead of California time. She doubted Alex would be in bed yet. Was he out with a beautiful woman tonight? And what if he was?

For a man she'd barely met, Dana couldn't believe how he'd gotten under her skin so fast. It was that unexpected invitation to dinner with him. He didn't have to take the time, but the fact that he did made him different from the other men she'd known. She found him not only remarkable, but disturbingly attractive.

While she finished the last of her peanut butter and jelly sandwich, she reached for her mother's favorite French cookbook from the shelf. It wasn't a cookbook exactly. It was a very delightful true story about an American family living in France in 1937. Quite by accident they met a French woman who came to cook for them.

Everything you ever wanted to know about France was in it, including French phrases. It was full of recipes and little drawings, so much better than a Michelin guide. Both Dana and her mom had read it many times, marveling over a slice of history captured in the account. Dana would pack this with her.

In the act of opening the cover, warm memories of her mother assailed her. A lump stayed lodged in her throat all the way to the bedroom where she flung herself on the bed to thumb through it. Chanzeaux looked just like the adorable villages in the book with their open-air markets selling the most amazing items. She rolled over on her back, wondering about Alex. Having lived on the other side of the world, did he find France as charming as she did?

There were many questions she'd like to ask him, but she'd already probed too much. Anything more she learned *he* would have to volunteer when they happened to see each other. He could be slightly forbidding. It would be wise to stay out of his way. That went for her father, too, except to feed him.

Oh, yes, and remind him to go to the local hospital for his weekly blood test. No one would believe what a baby he was, which reminded her she'd better check the medicine cabinet and make sure he had enough blood thinner medication to be gone two months. After they left

France, they'd finish up the filming in Germany where Dana had already checked out the locations ahead of time.

With a sigh she got up from the bed needing to do a dozen things, but a strong compulsion led her to the den first. Ever since she'd heard that the Fleury family had once produced wine, she wanted to learn what she could about it. The wine she'd had with Alex had left the taste of nectarines on her lips. As she'd told him that night, it could become addicting.

She typed in Anjou wine, France. Dozens of Web sites popped up. She clicked on the first one.

The Anjou is one of the subregions of the Loire Valley producing a variety of dry to sweet dessert wines. The two main regions for Chenin Blanc are found in Touraine and along the Layon river where the soil is rich in limestone and tuffeau. Long after you've tasted this wine, it will give up a stone-fruit flavor on the palate. The Dutch merchants in the sixteen hundreds traded for this wine.

That far back?

Fascinated by the information, Dana researched a little more.

Coteaux du Layon near the river is an area in Anjou where the vines are protected by the hills. It's best known for its sweet wines, some of the recipes going back fifteen centuries. By the late seventeen hundreds, several wine producers became dominant in the region including the Domaine du Rochefort, Domaine du Château Belles Fleurs and Domaine Percher.

There it was, part of Alex's family history. Dana's father would find the information riveting, as well, but for the meantime she'd keep it to herself. The owner was a private person. It would be best if she waited until he brought it up in the conversation, if he ever did.

A few minutes later she'd gone back to her room to do her packing. She had it down to a science, fitting everything into one suitcase. As she was about to leave and do some errands, her father came home and poked his head in the door. "There you are."

She looked up at him. "Hi."

"You just got back. How come you're packing again so soon?"

Dana had anticipated his question. "I'm going to fly to Paris with the camera guys in the morning."

"Why?"

"Because Saskia will be a lot happier if she

has you to herself when you fly out the day after tomorrow."

"Saskia doesn't run my life," he declared.

No one ran his life. Dana certainly didn't figure in it except to fetch for him, but the actress didn't like her. "I know that, but it doesn't hurt to keep the troops happy, does it?" She flashed him a smile, hoping to ease the tension, maybe provoke a smile, but all she provoked was a frown.

"You really think you found the right place?" he asked morosely.

The film was on his mind, nothing or no one else. Until he saw the estate, he'd be impossible to live with. Good luck to Saskia. "If I haven't, Paul will switch us back to Plan B outside Paris without problem."

After staring into space for another minute he said, "Have you seen my reading glasses?"

"They're on the kitchen counter, next to the script. Have you eaten?"

"I don't remember."

"I'll fix you some eggs and toast."

"That's a good girl," he muttered, before leaving her alone.

He only said that if he needed something from her. Because he was a narcissist, it was all she would get. She knew that, yet because their natures were exact opposites, a part of her would always want more. Still, when she thought of Alex's mother being cut off by her father, Dana realized her relationship with her father hadn't degenerated to that extent. Not yet…

Alex was in his bedroom when the phone rang again. He'd just hung up from talking with another Realtor who hadn't heard the estate wasn't for sale and never had been. They never stopped hounding him. With each call he'd hoped it might be Dana.

"Monsieur Martin *ici*."

"*Bonjour*, Alex."

His lips twitched. Her accent needed help, but with a grown-up rosebud mouth like hers, no Frenchman would care. "*Bonjour*, Dana. How are things in Hollywood?"

"I wouldn't know. How are things in that jungle of yours?"

Laughter burst out of him. "Prickly."

"My condolences."

"Where are you exactly?"

"In front of the château."

He felt a burst of adrenaline kick in.

"I was hoping you would let me in, but considering your plight, I'll be happy to come back after you and your machete have emerged."

The chuckles kept on coming. "I'm closer than you think. Don't go away." He hung up and strode swiftly through the foyer.

As soon as he opened the front door of the chateau, she got out of the car. Today she was dressed in jeans and a white short-sleeved top. If the pale blue vest she wore over it was meant to hide the lovely mold of her body, it failed.

Though she gave the appearance of being calm and collected, he noticed a pulse throbbing too fast at her throat. He knew in his gut she was glad to see him.

"When did you fly into Paris?"

"At six-thirty this morning with the camera guys. When their rooms are ready, they'll crash until tomorrow, then probably show up around eight in the morning to start checking things out."

"What about your father?"

"Everyone else will arrive at different times tomorrow."

"I see. He didn't mind you coming on ahead?"

"Most of the time we do our own thing." She gave him a direct glance as if daring him to contradict her.

Alex had asked enough questions for now.

It was almost noon. "Let's get you inside. In case you'd like to freshen up, there's a bathroom on the second floor at the head of the stairs."

"Thank you."

Dana followed him up the steps into the foyer dominated by the central stonework staircase. With no furniture, paintings, tapestries or rugs visible, the château was a mere skeleton, but she seemed mesmerized.

Taking advantage of her silence he said, "The place was denuded years ago. Everything is stored on the third level where the servants used to live."

He watched her eyes travel from the walls' decorative Italianate paneling to the inlaid wood floors. "There's a chandelier packed away that should hang over the staircase. Without it the château is dark at night. I told Paul that if night interiors are called for, he'll need to plan for extra lighting. Your father—"

"My father's very superstitious," she broke in on a different tack. "He gets that from his Swedish ancestry. When he stands where I'm standing, he'll be frightened at first."

"Frightened?"

"Yes." She turned to him. "It's always frightening for a figment of your imagination to come to life, don't you think? At first he won't know if it's a good or bad omen."

When her father saw the château, he would be speechless. His excitement wouldn't be obvious to the casual observer, but she'd see his eyes flicker and feel his positive energy radiate. For a while it would insulate him from his usual irritations. Even Saskia wouldn't grate on his nerves as much, at least not at first. But that was *his* problem. Dana had done her part.

"Would you mind being more explicit?" Everything she said intrigued Alex. Besides her shape and coloring that appealed strongly to his senses, she had an inquiring mind. It engendered an excitement inside him that was building in momentum.

"My father gave his favorite screen writer some ideas and they collaborated on the script for this wartime film. Your château and grounds could have been made for it. For some time I've had the feeling this is the most important project he's ever taken on."

He folded his arms. "Can you tell me about it, or is it a secret?"

"A secret? No." After a pause. "The film is filled with the kind of angst my father is best known for." He heard her breathe in deeply. "Does that explanation help?"

"About the setting, yes, but I'm curious about the story itself."

She gave a gentle shrug of her shoulders. "That's for my father to decide. I don't think he knows it all yet." As far as Alex was concerned, she was being evasive for a reason. "Dad's had a mind block lately. It's made him more irritable than usual. It will take settling into it here for those creative juices to flow again. But to give you a specific answer to your question, his films always leave the audience asking more questions."

That was the truth, but she was holding back from him and that made him more curious than ever. Evidently she knew better than to give too much away. Was that because her father wouldn't like it? "Why do you think he came up with this particular story?"

"How does any author come up with an idea? They see something, hear something that arouses their interest and a kernel of an idea starts to form."

She angled her head toward him. "Part of it could be the guilt he personally feels for his country's compliance with the enemy in the first days of World War II. Another part might be that deep down he still misses mother and wishes he'd had a son instead of '*moi*.'"

She'd said it with a smile, but Alex felt the words like a blow to the gut. He'd heard emptiness, sadness in that last remark. It made him want to comfort her. "Still, I have my uses. Thanks to you, I found *this* for him." She spread her hands, as if encompassing the entire château. "Heaven sent."

Alex swallowed hard. "For me, too."

"I'm happy if it helps you. I bet your mother is, too."

She kept surprising him. "You believe in heaven, Dana?"

"Yes. Don't you?"

"After this discussion, I want to."

A faint blush filled her cheeks. "I'm afraid I've rattled on too long and have kept you from your work. Please go ahead and do whatever you were doing. If it's all right, I'll just wander around here for a little while before I take a nap. I picked up a sleeping bag in Angers and brought it with me."

Why would she do that? "If you're that exhausted, I'll call the Hermitage and tell them to get your room ready now."

"No doubt they'd make concessions for you,

but I'm not staying there, so it's not necessary. Thank you anyway."

Alex rubbed the back of his neck in an unconscious gesture. "Paul told me he would arrange rooms there for you and your father."

"He already has, but while I'm in France I intend to be on my own most of the time. After everyone goes home at the end of the day's shoot, I plan to stay right here where I can have the whole château to myself."

An angry laugh escaped his throat. "I'm afraid that's impossible."

She flashed him an ingenuous smile. "Don't worry about me. I don't frighten easily and love being alone."

His eyes narrowed. Dana had seemed such an innocent she'd almost fooled him. "I'm afraid you don't understand," he ground out. "My ad didn't indicate the château could be used for anything but the filming."

A long silence ensued while she digested what he'd said. "I assumed that since the company had rented the estate for the filming, it wouldn't matter if I found myself a little spot in the château to sleep at night." Her supple body stiffened. "My mistake, Alex. I'm glad you cleared it up before any harm was done."

"Dana—"

She'd almost reached the front door before turning around. "Yes?"

He started toward her. "Where are you going?"

"To find me a place to stay."

"Wouldn't you be better off with your father?" he asked quietly.

"You want your pound of flesh, don't you." Her cheeks filled with angry color. "First of all, if I were seventeen I'd agree with you, but I'm going to be twenty-seven next week, slightly too long in the tooth to still be daddy's little girl."

His estimation of her age had been way off.

"Secondly, my father isn't in his dotage yet. In fact, his latest love interest is one of the actresses in the film and will be sleeping with him, which makes three a crowd. When you see Saskia, you'll understand a lot of things." She smiled. "If my dad ever found out your impression of him, he'd have a coronary."

Alex hadn't seen that one coming. It knocked him sideways.

"Thirdly, while I'm in this glorious region of France, I'd like to pretend I'm an independent woman who needs to spread her own wings for a change. It must have given you an uncomfortable moment thinking I'd made you my target. Again, I apologize."

He'd anticipated her flight and moved in time to prevent her from opening the door. Their hips brushed against each other in the process, increasing his awareness of her womanly attributes. The tension between them was palpable. She slowly backed away from him.

The last thing he'd wanted was to make an enemy of her, but that's what he'd done. One word to her father and he could kiss this deal goodbye. The hell of it was, he couldn't afford to lose this film studio's business, not when he needed the money so badly. A large portion of his life's savings combined with the modest inheritance from his father were all invested in this venture.

"Dana—it never occurred to me you might want to stay in the château."

She refused to look at him. "You're not a dreamer."

"You'd be surprised, but that's not the point." Trying to gauge what her reaction would be he said, "I live here."

Her gaze flew to his. By the stunned look in those blue depths, he knew instinctively his revelation had come as a surprise.

"The concierge at the Hermitage intimated you lived somewhere in the vicinity. To me that ruled out the château..." Her voice trailed.

Alex's first impression of the French woman in Chanzeaux had been right. She was a busybody. When Dana's father arrived and she learned of his importance, it would bring a flood of unwanted curiosity seekers to the estate. His mouth thinned in irritation. He would have to fit the gate with an electronic locking device to give the film company privacy while they were working. Today, if possible.

"I'm afraid there's been a lot of speculation about me since I flew in from Bali."

"Bali— What were you doing there?"

"My work. I'm an agricultural engineer."

She rubbed her palms against womanly hips, as if she didn't know what to do with them. "Are you taking a sabbatical of sorts then?"

"No. I resigned in order to settle mother's estate before leaving for the States."

Following his remark she said, "Then you're only in France temporarily."

"Very temporarily, even if my business venture should succeed—" he drawled.

"What is your plan exactly?"

"To restore the château and grounds to a

point that the estate can be put on display alongside the others in the area. Millions of tourists
pour into France each year willing to pay entry
fees for a look around. With a couple of full-
time caretakers, it could prove to be a smart
business investment, leaving me free to pursue
my career overseas."

Her expression had undergone a subtle change
he couldn't decipher. "It's an ambitious under-
taking, but with your work ethic I'm sure you'll
make it happen." She glanced at her watch. "I
need to go and let you get back to your work."

"Not so fast." He looked around before his
gaze centered on her once more. "It does seem
unconscionable not to let you live here when
this was originally built to house several dozen
people. Under the circumstances I *insist* you
stay, but it means we share the château."

CHAPTER THREE

INSIST?

The provocative statement was backed by a steel tone, making her tremble. It seemed Alex Martin had changed his mind and was willing to let her stay here. Not willing, she amended. Determined all of a sudden.

Why?

Maybe like Neal he could see himself making a lot more money to save the château if he starred in a film. He was gorgeous enough to be a top box office draw, yet the mere idea that he saw Dana as a stepping stone to influence her father made her so ill, she shuddered.

If she was wrong about his motive, then for the life of her she couldn't think what the reason might be. The man could have any woman he wanted.

Alex's dark brows knit together. "Why so reticent now?"

The question coming from his compelling mouth was like a challenge wrapped up in a deceptively silky voice. It curled around Dana's insides down to her toes. If she didn't have to think about it, the idea of being under the same roof with Alex Martin for the next three weeks was so thrilling, she was ready to jump out of her skin.

But she *did* have to think about it for all the usual reasons of propriety, common sense and self-preservation—self-preservation especially because he could be moody and overbearing like her father, the very thing she'd wanted to get away from for a while.

And then there were the unusual reasons, like the fact that her father was coming here to direct the most important film of his career on her say-so alone. If she made a misstep with Alex now and he decided to renege on the contract, how would she explain it to her dad, let alone the rest of the company?

Money had changed hands. Too much was at stake on both men's parts for there to be trouble at this stage because of her.

When she'd declared that she wanted to be an independent woman and spread her own wings, she'd set herself up to be taken at her word and

Alex had acted on it. He was probably laughing at her naïveté right now while he waited to hear that she'd changed her mind and didn't want to stay here after all.

The stakes were too high for her to turn this into a battle. An inner voice warned her there was wisdom in going along with him. Dana knew nothing like this would ever come her way again. Why not take him up on it? She wouldn't be human if she didn't avail herself of such an opportunity.

"Thank you, Alex. I'll do my best not to get underfoot." From now on she could fade into the shadows and be like Diane de Poitiers, Henri II's mistress at Chenonceau, who adored the château and oversaw the plantings of the flower and vegetable gardens.

Dana would glut herself on the history of Belles Fleurs, but wherever she slept, she would make certain it wasn't anywhere near Alex. When she'd called his château small, she'd meant it hadn't been built on the scale of Chambord with its 440 rooms, but it was big enough for her to get lost in.

An odd gleam in his dark eyes was the only sign that her answer had surprised him. "With that settled, shall we go upstairs? You can have your pick of any room on the second floor."

By tacit agreement they both started toward the magnificent staircase. "How many are there?"

"Six."

While she was wondering where his room was located, he read her mind. "For the time being I've made the petit salon off the main foyer into a combined bedroom and office for me."

They'd be a floor apart. That was good. Of course when she wanted to go out for any reason, he'd be aware of her leaving through the front door, that is *if* and *when* he was around. After a few days of becoming aware of his routine, she'd make sure not to disturb him any more than she could help.

When they reached the long vestibule, she was overwhelmed by what she saw. "This is similar to the rib-vaulting at Chenonceau! It's utterly incredible!"

Alex nodded. "On a much smaller scale of course." She was conscious of his tall, hard-muscled frame as he continued walking to one end of the corridor on those long, powerful legs. "Let's start with the bedroom in the turret round."

"Oh—" she cried the second he opened the door and she took everything in. "This is the one I want!"

A smile broke the corner of his sensuous

mouth. "You're sure? You haven't seen the others yet. The turret round on the other end has a fireplace."

"I'm positive. Look at these!" There were fleur-de-lis designs placed at random in the inlaid wood flooring. She got down on her knees to examine them.

"If the original designer of this château could see a modern-day woman like you studying his intricate workmanship this closely, he would be delighted by the sight."

"Go ahead and mock me," she said with a laugh before getting to her feet. For the next few minutes she threw her head back to study the cross-beamed ceiling. There were little white enamel ovals rimmed in gold placed every so often in the wood depicting flowers and various forest creatures. "How did they do that? How did they do any of this?"

She darted to the window that needed washing inside and out, but at least it wasn't broken. The entire room would require a good scrubbing to get rid of layers of accumulated dust. Even so there was a fabulous view of the countryside and a certain enchanted feel about the room. Eventually she turned to him. "Do you think this might have been your mother's?"

Her question seemed to make him more pensive and probably brought him pain. She wished she'd caught herself before blurting it out.

"My mother lived here until her early twenties. I have no idea which bedroom she occupied, but it wouldn't surprise me if it had been this one. The view of the Layon from the window at this angle is surreal."

"I noticed," Dana murmured. "I'm glad she met your father so she wasn't so lonely anymore."

Alex shifted his weight. "*Lonely* is an interesting choice of words."

"She would have been, wouldn't she? To know her father preferred her brother?"

"I'm sure you're right," he muttered. "Mother often seemed melancholy, at least that's what I called it, but you've hit on a better description. Even in a crowded room she sometimes gave off a feeling of loneliness that no doubt troubled my father, too."

"Forgive me for saying anything, Alex. It's none of my business. It must be the atmosphere here getting to me."

"You *are* your father's daughter after all, so it's understandable." She didn't detect anything more than slight amusement in his tone, thank heaven.

"If you'll tell me where to find some cleaning

supplies, I'll get started in here before I bring up my sleeping bag."

He tilted his dark head. "I have a better idea. We'll drive into Angers in my truck and eat lunch. I need to pick up some items. While we're there, we'll get you a new mattress and box springs."

"You don't need to do that."

"I wouldn't allow you to stay here in a sleeping bag. After we come back, we'll clean the room together and I'll bring down a few pieces of furniture from storage. By sunset Rapunzel will be safely ensconced in her tower."

She chuckled to hide her excitement at spending the day with him, not to mention the rest of the month. "You're mixing up your fairy tales. I don't have long hair."

He gave an elegant shrug of his broad shoulders. "It's evident you haven't read the definitive version. Her father had her long golden tresses cut off so no prince could climb up to her."

A few succinct words dropped her dead in her tracks. In the tale Dana had grown up with, there'd been a wicked witch. Was he still teasing her, or had this tale suddenly taken on a life of its own. "Then how did the prince reach her?"

He paused in the doorway. "I guess you'll have to read the end of the story to find out."

His cryptic explanation was no help.

"I'll bring the truck around. When you've freshened up, meet me outside. I'll lock the door with my remote."

When she left the château a few minutes later, Alex was lounging against a blue pickup loaded with cut off branches and uprooted clumps of weeds. Dana marveled that he did this kind of backbreaking work without help. Pruning the grounds would be a Gargantuan task for half a dozen teams of gardeners, but he couldn't afford to hire help because the taxes were eating him alive.

She felt his dark fringed eyes wander over her as she came closer. They penetrated, causing her pulse to race. Still, everything would have been all right for the trip into town if their bodies hadn't brushed while he helped her inside the cab. Her breath caught and she feared he'd noticed. With nowhere to run, she had to sit there and behave like she didn't feel electrified.

"This won't take long," he said a few minutes later, jolting her out of her chaotic thoughts. They'd stopped at a landfill to dump the debris. Fortunately there was a man there ready to help him, making short work of it. Soon they were on their way again.

After driving this route several times already, Dana recognized some of the landmarks leading into Angers. The massive castle dominating the town on the Maine came into view.

"Have you been through it?"

She shook her head. "Not yet, but I plan to. What about you?"

"One look at the condition of the estate and any thoughts I had of playing tourist flew out the broken windows."

Dana flicked him a sideward glance. "You know what that old proverb says about Jack working all the time."

He surprised her by meeting her gaze head-on. "Are you by any chance intimating I'm a dull boy?"

"Maybe not dull…" Dana said, before she wished she hadn't.

"You can't leave me hanging now—" It came out more like a growl, but he was smiling. When he did that, he was transformed into the most attractive man she'd ever seen or met. There was no sign of the boy he would have once been, one probably not as carefree with a mother whose heart had been broken.

"As you reminded me earlier, you'll have to read to the end of the story to find out."

"Touché."

Dana was glad when he turned onto a side street and pulled up near a sidewalk café full of locals and tourists. She slid out of the cab before he could come around to help her.

There was one empty bistro table partially sheltered from the sun by an umbrella. Alex escorted her to it before anyone else grabbed it. The temperature had been mild earlier, but now it was hot. A waiter came right over and took their orders for sandwiches.

Alex eyed her. "I could use a cup of coffee, but maybe you'd prefer something cold. The air's more humid than usual today."

"Coffee sounds fine." The waiter nodded and disappeared. She sat back in her chair. "I thought most French people preferred tea."

"I grew up on coffee."

"No billy tea?" she teased, referring to his Aussie roots.

He shook his head, drawing her attention to the hair brushing his shirt collar. In the light she picked out several shades ranging from dark brown to black. "I'm afraid tea doesn't do it for me."

"Nor me." She smiled. "You seem so completely French, I forgot."

"It's a good thing *my* father isn't around to hear that."

After a brief silence she said, "When you want to go home, that's a long flight."

"I have no home in the traditional sense. My father's work took us many places. We globe-trotted. Mother died in the Côte D'Ivoire and father on Bali where we were both working for the same company at the time. They're buried in Brisbane."

Dana took a deep breath. "Well, you have a home now."

One dark eyebrow lifted. "A liability you mean. I'm not certain it's worth it."

She wished she could lighten his mood. "That's right. You have other plans. Where in the States?"

"Louisiana. It's where my particular expertise, such as it is, can be fully utilized."

"Are you in such a hurry then?"

The waiter served them their order before Alex responded. "I wasn't aware of it, but I suppose I am."

While he made inroads on the ham and cheese melt, she took a sip of the hot liquid. "Sounds like your father's lifestyle rubbed off on you."

The gaze he flicked her was surprisingly

intense. "From the little you've told me about yourself, I'd say you've been similarly afflicted."

"Afflicted?" An odd choice of word. She stopped munching on her first bite. Of course she understood what he meant. Years of traveling around Europe finding locations for her father prevented her from staying in one spot. But it didn't mean that under the right circumstances, she couldn't settle down quite happily.

"Some people never leave the place they were born," he murmured. "I'm not so sure they haven't figured out life's most important secret."

She chuckled. "You mean, while nomads like us wander to and fro in search of what we don't know exactly?"

An amused glint entered his dark eyes. "Something like that."

"Well, given a choice, I'm glad I'm the way I am. Otherwise I wouldn't be living this fantasy. My own little girl dreams of being a princess in a castle in a far-off land have come true. Never mind that it will all end in a month, I intend to enjoy every minute of it now, thanks to your generosity."

Aware she'd been talking too much, she ate the rest of her sandwich.

"You think that's what it is?" The question

sent her pulse off the charts. "Little boys have their fantasies, too," came the wicked aside.

Fingers of warmth passed through her body. "My mother taught me they're not for a little girl's ears." After drinking the last of her coffee she dared a look at him. "Just how young did you think I was when we first met?"

"Too young," was all he was willing to reveal. He put some money on the table and stood up. "If you're ready we'll get some serious shopping done. Groceries last, I think."

She would pay for her keep, she thought to herself. He might be letting her sleep at the château, but she didn't expect anything else.

After visiting a hardware store, he took her to the third floor of the department store where the mattresses were sold. Alex sought out the male clerk and they conversed in French. Their speech was so rapid she understood nothing. Within a few seconds the younger man looked at her and broke out in a broad smile.

"I don't think I want a translation," she told Alex.

His lips curved upward. "You don't need to worry. When he asked me what kind of a mattress we were looking for, I simply asked him if he knew the story of the Princess and the Pea. He said he had the ideal one for you."

She tried not to laugh. "I see."

The clerk spread his hands in typical French fashion. "Would Mademoiselle like to try it?"

"She says yes," Alex spoke for her. They followed the man across the floor to the sample mattresses on display.

"This one is the best. *S'il vous plait.* Lie down."

"Don't be shy," Alex whispered. "He's not Figaro measuring a space for your marriage bed."

An imp got into Dana. "Maybe he thinks he's measuring yours. Why don't you try it first and humor him?"

With enviable calm Alex stretched out on one side of it, putting his hands behind his handsome head. Through shuttered eyes he stared up at her, jump-starting her heart.

"*Venez, mademoiselle.*" The clerk patted the other side. "He said you needed a double bed. See how you fit."

You said you wanted to spread your wings, Dana Lofgren. But she hadn't anticipated literally spreading out on a bed next to Alex for all creation to see. Several people on the floor had started watching with embarrassing interest. If she waited any longer, she'd turn this into a minor spectacle.

Once she'd settled herself full length against the mattress, she turned her head to Alex. "How does it feel against your sore back?"

He rolled on his side toward her, bringing him breathtakingly close. "You noticed." His voice sounded deep and seductive just then.

Afraid he knew that she noticed everything about him, she said, "I think we should take it. Look—even this close to me, the mattress doesn't dip."

"I noticed." This time when he spoke, she felt his voice reach right down inside to her core. The way his eyes had narrowed on her mouth, she slid off the bed in reaction and got to her feet on shaky legs.

"Eh bien, mademoiselle?"

She decided to make his day. "It's perfect"

He rubbed his hands together. "Excellent."

"Alex? I'll go to the linen department for the bedding. Meet you at the truck." Without looking at him, she made her way down to the next floor.

When the saleswoman asked what Dana had in mind, she described the beamed ceiling. "There's a mini print wallpaper of gold fleurs-de-lis on a cranberry field. I'd like to follow through with those colors."

"I have the exact thing for you."

Within minutes Dana left the store with a new pillow, pale cranberry sheets and bath towels with tiny gold fleurs-de-lis, a cranberry duvet and matching pillow sham.

Alex had reached the truck ahead of her. Together with two other men from the warehouse, he put the boxes with the mattress and box springs in the back. Upon her approach, he plucked the items right out of her arms with effortless male grace. While he stowed them, she climbed in the cab, eager to get back to the château and make up her new bed.

Without her having to say anything, he drove straight to a boulangerie where she salivated before loading up on nummy little quiches and ham-filled croissants. Alex bought three baguettes and several tranches of Gruyère and Camembert cheese.

"I already feel debauched and haven't even tasted a morsel yet," she moaned the words.

On the way back to the truck his eyes swerved to hers with a devilish glitter. "That's the whole idea. Earlier today I was accused of being a dull boy."

She quivered. If he got any duller, her heart wouldn't be able to take it. "I might have exaggerated a little."

"Careful, Mademoiselle Lofgren, or I'll get the impression you're trying to kill me with kindness." He turned on the engine and they took off.

She'd never had so much fun in her life and the day wasn't over yet.

"I'm coming down the hall, Dana. I hope you're ready."

He couldn't tell if she cried in fear or giggled. "Alex—please— It's almost ten o'clock. You've done enough! I don't need anything more." They'd cleaned every inch of the room until it gleamed. She was so genuinely appreciative of everything he did for her, it made him want to do more.

"I think you'll find this to be of comfort." Using his high-powered flashlight so he could see, he entered the turret round and put the heavy bronze floor candelabra near the head of the bed he'd brought down from storage. It was as tall as she was.

Dana held her own flashlight to guide him. She'd taken off her shoes and was in a kneeling position on top of her newly made bed. Using his automatic lighter, he lit the twelve candles in their sconces. Like the sun coming up over the horizon, the room slowly filled with flickering, mellow light.

"Oh—" she cried softly.

His sentiments exactly. The candles illuminated not only the inlaid woods of the Italian armoire and dresser, but the utterly enchanting female who'd worked hard right alongside him all afternoon and evening. Her peaches-and-cream complexion glowed, causing her blue eyes to dazzle him.

"The candles will burn down in an hour or so. Enough time to do some reading before jet lag takes over."

She shut off her flashlight. "I think I'm in a time warp."

"I feel that way every time I come inside the château." *Get out of her bedroom. Now.* "Before I go downstairs, we'd better discuss how you want to handle your father tomorrow."

Something in her eyes flickered that had nothing to do with the candlelight. "What do you mean handle?"

"I thought it was obvious. Sweet dreams, princess."

* * *

Dana had no agenda. No place she had to be.

After sleeping in until noon, she spent a long time in the modern bathtub, studying everything. She marveled at the superb job Alex had done of combining contemporary and eighteenth-century decor.

The tile work of the ancient looking floor . had been laid in a stunning, stone-green and white checkerboard design. Her eyes followed the lines of the green border also carried out around the window and the door.

Delighted by every inch of work created by a master craftsman, she was loathe to leave her bath. However, the pads of her fingers resembled prunes. Without electricity to blowdry her hair up here, she needed to towel it some more, then brush it dry before she went downstairs.

An ornate, mural-size mirror with a rococo-style gilt frame hung on the wall opposite the tub, another sybaritic element of the château. A gasp escaped her lips when she stood up and saw herself reflected full-size. She had a mirror on the back of the door at home, but it was in her bedroom and seemed miniscule in comparison.

One more look at herself was a reminder that

only a few days of enjoying the food they'd bought and she'd put on five pounds just like that!

Discipline, Dana. Self-control.

On the way back to the room in her robe, she repeated the motto that went for other things besides food. Like other people for instance. No, not other people. Just one person.

She clutched the lapels of her robe tighter. *A man like no one else.*

When she entered the room she could hear her phone vibrating on the dresser. Maybe it was Alex wondering if she was still alive. Suddenly breathless, she clicked on with a smile. *"Bonjour!"*

"Is that you, Dana?"

Her father's voice. What a surprise! "Hi, Dad. How was the flight?" He hated being closed in for long periods.

"Boring." That meant his girlfriend hadn't been able to keep him distracted.

"And Saskia?"

"She's at the Metropole in Angers."

"You sound tired. Where are you exactly?"

"I'm standing in my room at the Hermitage," he grumbled. "More to the point, where are you? The concierge said you never came in last night." He actually noticed?

"That's right. I've decided to stay at the château. It will save me a lot of coming and going."

Alex had the strange idea she was under her father's thumb. If he only knew the truth, that her father didn't think much about her at all. There was nothing to handle, but her host had insinuated something else and it rankled.

"I thought it was deserted."

"Not completely." She started brushing her hair. "The owner lives here. He's been very accommodating and made an allowance for me. After you've slept a few hours, drive over to the château in your rental car and I'll meet you at the gate."

There was a noticeable silence, then he said, "I'm coming now."

Clearly he couldn't wait to see if she'd pulled through for him. Everything hinged on her find.

"In that case let me go over the directions with you." Without Saskia in tow, he could walk around and think in peace. "See you shortly."

Once she'd pulled on jeans and a short-sleeved cotton top in an aqua color, she finished doing her hair and put on lipstick. Slipping her feet into her favorite leather sandals, she grabbed her phone and left the room. Later, after her father had gotten a feel for the estate, she would feed him a late lunch in the kitchen before he went back to the hotel.

Last evening she'd only had a brief glimpse of the salon. Today the door was closed. Alex could be inside at the computer, but in all probability he was out hacking away at his private jungle.

This was the way it should be. Out of sight, out of mind. Didn't she wish!

She stepped out into a day that seemed hotter than yesterday, but she hadn't noticed because the interior of the château was cooler. It felt like being in a cathedral to walk beneath the trees. Here and there sunlight dappled their branches.

As she continued on, the crunch of her feet on the leaves must have startled some squirrels. They chattered before she saw them scamper up a trunk and disappear. She was still laughing in pure pleasure when she came upon Alex at the gate.

He was down on his haunches in jeans and another thin white T-shirt, fastening something to the wrought iron. She could see the play of muscle across his shoulders. Her heart thudded so hard she was positive he could hear it.

"Sleeping Beauty at last," he murmured, scrutinizing her from head to toe with eyes so dark and alive this afternoon, it sent a delicious current of desire through her body.

"You're getting your princesses mixed up."

"No—" He went back to fastening a screw with his power drill. "You're a woman of many parts. I never know which one is going to emerge at any given moment."

His comment produced a smile from her. "You're full of it, Alex, but keep it up. By the time I leave here, I'll be taking a whole host of enchanting memories with me."

His hands stilled for a moment. "Where are you going next?"

"To a little town on the Rhine in Germany for a month where the last segment of the film will be made."

He dusted himself off and got to his feet. "Stand back and let's see if I've done this right." Pulling a remote from his pocket, he pressed the button. The gate took its time, but it clanged shut.

"*Bravo*. Too bad you didn't get to work on it sooner. It would have kept me out and forced me to phone you for an appointment."

Before she could take another breath, he shot her a laserlike glance. "As you've already surmised, I didn't mind the surprise or you wouldn't be living here." His comment filled her body with warmth. "But I've decided this was necessary to keep out trespassers while the studio is filming every day." He tossed her the remote. "It's yours. I have more in the office I'll give to Paul for anyone who needs one."

"Thank you."

She felt his gaze linger on her features. "Were you looking for me?"

Dana sucked in her breath. "No. My father's on his way over from the hotel. I told him I'd meet him here."

As if talking about him conjured him up, a red rental car appeared and came to a halt. Before Alex said anything that would remind her of his parting words last night, she pressed the button on the remote and the gate swung open.

"Hi, Dad. Drive on through."

He nodded his balding head and did her bidding. Once he'd passed through, he stopped the car and got out. Solid, yet lithe, he'd dressed in his favorite gray work slacks and matching crew neck shirt. His blue eyes, several shades darker than hers, gave them both a stare that others might consider fierce, but Dana was used to it.

"Dad, I'd like you to meet Monsieur Alexandre Martin, the owner of the estate."

"Monsieur." The two men shook hands.

"Call me Alex. I've seen several of your films which I found remarkable. It's a privilege to meet you."

"Thank you. Your English is excellent."

"He's part Australian, Dad."

"Ah. That explains the particular nuance I couldn't identify."

"Unlike your accent in English that no one could ever mistake for anything but Svenska," Dana quipped.

"Too true." His hooded gaze darted back and forth between her and Alex before he addressed him. "My daughter has convinced me I won't be disappointed with this location."

Alex eyed her father through veiled eyes. "Why don't you take a walk down this road alone. The left fork will bring you to the front of the château. The door's unlocked. Take all the time you want wandering around. I understand you'd rather do the discovering than be herded."

Dana's father looked stunned. That was because Alex had taken his cue from her. Among his many qualities, he'd just shown he was a master psychologist.

"Hand me the car keys, Dad. I'll drive it to the front courtyard and join you in a few minutes."

His surprised glance switched to her before

he dropped them in her hand. After nodding to Alex, he turned and began jogging.

Once he'd disappeared around the curve in the driveway, she turned to Alex who'd started gathering up his tools. She could tell he was anxious to get back to his pruning. Considering he'd spent all day yesterday and last evening seeing to it she had a bedroom worthy of a princess to sleep in, she didn't want to be the reason he was kept from his work any longer.

As soon as she'd climbed in the car, she poked her head out the window. "You handled my father brilliantly, Alex. Congratulations on being one of the few." The last thing she saw was his dark, enigmatic glance as she started the engine.

Get going, Dana!

Afraid if she stayed any longer she'd end up blurting out something incriminating like, did he want help? she followed the driveway while studiously avoiding looking at him through the rearview mirror.

After pulling up next to her rental car parked in front, she gave her father a few more minutes lead before she got out. This was one time she was so confident of his positive reaction, it shocked her when he suddenly emerged from the château with a face devoid of animation.

The look she'd expected to see in his eyes wasn't there.

"Follow me back to the Hermitage. We have to talk."

CHAPTER FOUR

ALEX was up in one of the tallest trees, cutting away dead branches, when he saw both cars leave the estate. Jan Lofgren couldn't have been on the premises more than ten minutes. That was quick, but Alex guessed he wasn't surprised. In less time, Dana had made the decision to rent the estate on behalf of the company.

His opinion of her father had been correct before meeting him. He personified conceit. Dana miraculously had none.

Two hours later, Alex was coming back from the landfill after another haul when his cell phone rang. Paul Soleri was calling to make sure he and the crew could get in. They were on their way to the estate.

The timing couldn't be better. Once Alex could welcome them and answer any questions, he'd resume his work. The knowledge that

Dana would be coming back to sleep after dark never left his mind.

Before long a car and two minivans pulled up in the front courtyard. Alex stepped out of the château to meet Paul and the dozen light and camera technicians assembled. They all appeared delighted by what they saw. Their enthusiasm escalated as they entered the château.

After Alex introduced himself and pointed out the location of the bathroom facilities, he told them to look around and explore all they wanted. Except for the petit salon on the main floor and the west turret round on the first floor, everything else was available to them.

If they wanted to do any filming in the building housing the winepress or down in the wine cellar beneath the château, they were welcome. Already he could tell they were getting ideas as they left the foyer and darted from room to room checking things out.

Paul, who was probably in his midforties, took him aside. "Has Jan been here yet?"

"Yes. A few hours ago. He didn't stay long, then he left with his daughter."

The dark blond man pursed his lips. "I'm surprised I haven't heard from him yet."

"Perhaps he was tired from the long flight."

"That's not like him," he mused. "I assumed he'd be here."

"I have to admit I thought it strange he left in such a hurry," Alex commented.

"It doesn't matter." A pleasant smile broke out on his face. "We'll go ahead without him."

"Make yourself at home, Paul. As I told you over the phone, all the furniture is stored on the third floor. Nothing's locked. Use whatever you need."

He let out a long whistle. "When David gets here, he'll be floored."

"David?"

"The scriptwriter for this film. He'll be arriving any minute with the set designer and staff from costumes and makeup. They're all going to swoon."

"And that's good?"

"You have no idea. Since Jan wanted something unique for this segment of the film, we've been worried it didn't exist. Only Dana could pull this off. She's always had an instinct for picking the right places for him, but this time she outdid herself.

"Don't quote me, but she'll end up being a more brilliant director than her father."

That piece of information came totally unexpected. "Is directing one of her aspirations?"

"Yes, but the last person to know it is Jan, and that's another good thing."

Alex remembered her answer when he'd asked what she did in her spare time. *Nothing of report. I read and play around with cooking. Otherwise my father forgets to eat.*

"If you'll excuse me, Paul, I have to get back to my work outside. Phone if you need me."

"Will do."

Inexplicably disturbed by what he'd learned, he strode down the hallway leading to the side entrance of the château. Dana had been emphatic about not wanting to be an actress. Now it seemed Paul had supplied him with a viable reason.

Inherited talent happened on occasion, but he had the distinct feeling it would take uncommon courage for her to step out from Jan Lofgren's legendary shadow. When she did break out, she'd be caught up in her own career. The thought caused Alex to grind his teeth.

Dana found a parking space outside the Hermitage and followed her dad inside to his room. On the short drive from the château she'd prepared herself to hear that he wasn't pleased with her find.

She knew the place was perfect for the script, so it had to be something else he objected to. For the life of her she didn't know what it was. That meant his mood had already turned wretched and the whole company would pay for it. If she knew Paul, he'd already assembled the crew over there to get to work.

It would be bad enough if they had to pack up again and leave for the Paris location, but there was Alex to think about. The contract Sol had sent him was standard. There was a clause that said Alex would only receive a percentage of the money if for any reason they chose not to film there after all. That wasn't nearly enough compensation for him.

By the time she entered the hotel room, she was ready to fight her father. If he was going to pull out of this deal due to one of his mystical whims, then she would insist Alex be paid all the money agreed upon in good faith.

As usual his room was a mess, but for once she didn't start automatically straightening things. Instead she shut the door and propped her back against it. While she waited for him to speak first, she folded her arms.

He stood next to the dresser, eyeing her while he lit up a cigarette, almost as if he were daring her to protest. She couldn't remember the last time she'd seen him smoke. Her mother had begged him to stop. As a concession to her, he'd cut down a lot. Dana had hoped he would find the strength to quit altogether. Unfortunately Saskia smoked, too. Dana guessed it was asking too much.

"Tell me about Monsieur Martan." He pronounced Alex's last name the French way.

A red flag went up.

Months ago her father had started out another conversation in the same manner, only the subject in question had been Neal Robeson.

So… This was about Alex—not about the suitability of the château. Relief flooded her body.

No doubt when Alex had told her father to go ahead and explore on his own because of something Dana had confided, he hadn't liked it. She knew her dad enjoyed being a mystery to other people, so it had made him uncomfortable to be more transparent to Alex because of her. That irritation would pass, particularly since Alex wouldn't be around while her father worked.

"Martin is his Australian name," she corrected him.

With one long exhale, the room filled with smoke. "He must want to get into acting very badly to give me free rein to his entire estate."

She moved away from the door. "Have you forgotten I went to him, not the other way around? He wants money very badly to restore the château and make it a viable asset before he resumes his career as an agricultural engineer."

Her father gave her one of those condescending nods. "So that's what he's told you."

Dana refused to let him get to her. "In this case you're not dealing with another Neal type."

"No," he muttered, "Monsieur Martan is older and has far more worldly experience. Inside that supposedly deserted château with no electricity beyond the main floor, your bedchamber has been laid out so exquisitely, it even took *my* breath."

She scoffed. "Careful, Dad. You're beginning to make this sound like Beauty and the Beast. When I told him I was planning to stay there at night in my new sleeping bag, he insisted I have a decent bedroom."

He stubbed out his cigarette. "I forbid it, Dana."

Forbid? "I think you've forgotten I passed eighteen a long time ago." As she turned to leave, she heard knocking on the door.

"Jan? It's Saskia. Let me in, *lieveling*."

The timing was perfect, but her father looked ready to throw something.

"I'll get it," Dana volunteered before opening it.

"Hi, Saskia. Did you have a good flight?"

"So-so." The brunette actress kissed her on both cheeks, a pretense at civility.

Dana went along with to keep the peace.

"I was just leaving. See you later, Dad."

Without hesitation she rushed out of the hotel. It didn't take her long to reach the château.

By the time she'd pulled up next to the cars and minivans parked in front, Dana realized there'd be no peace for her if her father was angry enough to renege on the contract. Alex didn't deserve it, not to mention everyone else who would be put out. It looked like it was up to her if she didn't want this boat to sink.

When she found Alex and told him she wouldn't be staying at the château after all, he would assume it was what he'd thought from the first—that she still answered to her father in everything. But as humiliating as that would be, it wouldn't matter if it meant Alex received all his money.

"Dana?"

She got out of the car in time to see David hurrying toward her from the woods. He was her father's age, a wonderful family man with a great gift for writing.

When he caught up to her, he hugged her hard. "Bless you, Dana. Bless you, bless you for this. Words can't describe."

"I know." She'd felt the same way after seeing the château for the first time. It was how she felt now, only more so. He finally let her go, still beaming.

David's reaction settled it. This film was of vital importance to him, too; therefore she had no choice but to pack up her things and drive to the Hermitage. She checked her watch. It was ten to six. Pretty soon everyone would leave for the night. That's when she'd go inside to get her things so she wouldn't draw attention to herself.

Until then she would walk around the back of the château to find Alex. After what he'd done for her, she owed him an explanation of why she wouldn't be staying here after all. He would never know that because of him, she'd experienced the most exciting day and night of her entire life. A man like him was too good for her, but at least this was a memory she'd hug to herself forever.

After telling David she'd see him later, she followed the path next to the hedge at the side of the château. It led around to the back where she hadn't been before. To her surprise the ground, covered by a mass of tangled vegetation divided by a path, sloped gently toward the river.

She wandered down it a few feet, marveling at the sight. Alex had meticulously cleaned out one half of it to reveal individual fruit trees. Who would have guessed what had been hidden there? In its day, the grounds would have been a showplace.

The other part still needed to be tackled, but he was making inroads. She saw his truck piled with cleared-out vegetation. Nearby were various tools including a power saw.

"Bonsoir, ma belle."

Her heart raced. "Alex?" She'd heard his deep, seductive voice, but couldn't see him anywhere.

"I'm in a tree!" He tossed something small and green at her feet.

She reached for it, then looked up. A long, tall ladder had been propped against the trunk. Hidden by masses of leaves, she only saw parts of his hard-muscled physique. He brushed a few aside, allowing her a glimpse of his disarming white smile. Dana could hardly breathe.

"Are these all apple trees?"

"*Blanc d'Hiver* apples," he asserted. "The kind that make the best *tartes aux pommes*. By late October I might be able to harvest a few. The trees behind you yield Anjou pears."

Dana shook her head. "No wonder this place is called Belles Fleurs. When their blossoms come out, the sight from the château windows will be glorious.

"That all depends if I live long enough to make it out of this primeval forest to prune another day."

She chuckled. "How old are you?" She'd been dying to know.

"Thirty-three."

"You've got years yet!"

"Years of what?"

"I'm sure I don't know." Dana didn't want to think about his life when he moved on to other places. Other women… It would take a very special woman to capture his heart. "Tell me something—"

"That covers a lot of territory."

Laughter escaped her lips. "Can you see the vineyard from that altitude?"

"So you noticed the building housing the winepress."

"Yes, but I also heard that the vineyard once produced the famed Domaine Belles Fleurs label."

She heard the leaves rustle. In seconds he'd negotiated the ladder with swift male agility before jumping to the ground, carrying his hand saw. "Someone's been gossiping." He gathered the branches he'd just cut and threw them in the truck bed. "Wait, let me guess—Madame Fournier at the Hermitage."

Nothing got past him. "Who else?" She smiled, but he didn't reciprocate.

"Since my arrival, word has leaked out that a long-lost Fleury is back in Les Coteaux du Layon. It sounds like she was talking out of school again."

Dana had irritated him again; the last thing she'd wanted to do. "Only because I wanted to buy a bottle of the dessert wine we drank the other evening. She told me it came from the Domaine Percher, but she added that the very best Anjou wine used to come from the Domaine Belles Fleurs."

Alex rubbed his thumb along his lower lip. "There hasn't been a bottle produced since 1930."

"That's what she said. Naturally I was curious."

"Naturally," he came back, but to her relief he sounded more playful than upset.

"When I flew back to California, I did a little research on the Internet."

His eyes narrowed on her features. "What did you find out?"

"For one thing, Dutch merchants used to favor the Belles Fleurs brand."

He expelled a breath. "I might as well hear the rest. Knowing Dana Lofgren, you didn't stop there."

Embarrassed to be rattling on, a wave of heat washed over her. "There isn't any more, though I will say this—I'm no connoisseur, but if the Belles Fleurs wine was as good as the kind we had at the Hermitage, then it's the world's loss."

She noticed him shift his weight. "My parents never breathed a word to me about a vineyard."

"You're kidding!"

"My father was so intent on protecting my mother from any more pain, we simply didn't talk about her past. When the letter from the attorney for my grandfather's estate showed up, there was no mention of a vineyard. In fact, he led me to believe the place was virtually unsalvageable."

"Sounds like he was hoping you would forfeit so he could buy it for a song."

He nodded. "I got the distinct impression he was hiding something, but didn't understand until I saw the winepress building and eventually discovered the vineyard. No doubt he'd been bombarded by vintners throughout the Anjou region who wanted to buy it and work it, even if they couldn't afford to purchase the château."

"So he thought he'd buy it first," she theorized, "recognizing the money it could bring in."

"Exactly."

"Is it supposed to be a secret then?"

He put his hands on his hips, unconsciously emanating a potent virility that made her tremble. "Not at all."

"But you wish I'd mind my own business."

"You misunderstand me, Dana. There's something you *don't* know. Come with me while I make this last haul and I'll explain."

His invitation made it possible for her to be with him a little longer. She couldn't ask for more than that, but he paused before his next comment ruined the moment. "Unless of course your assistance is required elsewhere." His brow had furrowed. "Naturally your father has first call on your time."

Between Alex and her dad, she felt like a football being tossed back and forth. Both of them treated her like she was a child who couldn't act for herself. She'd thought she and

Alex had been communicating like two adults just now, but she'd thought wrong!

Bristling with the heat of anger she muttered, "If that were the case, I wouldn't have come out here, would I?"

Turning on her heel, she started to retrace her steps, but Alex moved faster. In the next breath his hands had closed around her upper arms, pulling her back against his chest. "Why *did* you come?" he asked in a silky voice.

With his warm breath against her neck, too many sensations bombarded her at once. The solid pounding of his heart changed the momentum of hers. Aware of his fingers making ever-increasing rotations against her skin through her top, she felt a weakness attack her body. Pleasure pains ran down her arms to her hands.

"I—I wanted to thank you." She could hardly get the words out.

"For what?" he demanded, turning her around, causing her head to loll back. His dark gaze pierced hers. "That sounded like you're leaving on a trip. Mind telling me where you're going?"

"The landfill? It may be a French one, but I can still think of more romantic places."

"Dana." His voice grated.

Of course he already knew the answer to his

own question, but his male mouth was too close. Her ache for him had turned into painful desire. She needed to do something quick before she forgot what they were talking about.

"I should have taken your advice before you went to so much trouble for me." She tried to ease away from him, but he didn't relinquish his hold. "My only consolation is that it's one room less you'll have to clean and furnish once you get started on the inside of the château."

Those black eyes roved over her features with increasing intensity. "You knew your father wasn't going to approve. What's changed?"

Dana moistened her lips nervously. "Remember the old saying about picking your battles?" She noticed a small nerve throbbing at the corner of his mouth. In other circumstances she'd love to press her lips to it. "This one isn't important."

She kept trying for a little levity, hoping it would help. It didn't. Her comment had the opposite effect of producing a smile. Some kind of struggle was going on inside him before his hands dropped away with seeming reluctance.

This was the moment to make her exit. "See you around, Alex."

Needing to put distance between them, she went back to the château to pack. It had emptied except for Paul and David. While they were talking in the grand salon, she hurried out to the car with her suitcase and headed for the hotel.

The same woman she'd talked to before smiled at her. "*Bonsoir*, Mademoiselle Lofgren."

"*Bonsoir, madame*. I need the key to room eleven, please."

Her arched brow lifted. "Eleven? But it is already occupied."

"I know. My father and I have adjoining rooms."

"*Non, non*. A Mademoiselle Brusse checked in a little while ago. I've already given her the key."

Something strange was going on.

"I see. Thank you for your help, *madame*."

"Of course."

Dana grabbed her suitcase and opted for the stairs rather than the lift. Once she reached the next floor, she walked midway down the hall and knocked on her father's door several times, but he didn't answer. No doubt he was with Saskia, but this couldn't wait. She pulled out her cell phone and called him.

"Dana?" He'd picked up on the second ring.

"Hi, Dad. What's going on? I tried to check in my room, but the desk said Saskia had picked up the key."

He answered her question with another one. "Where are you?"

"Standing in front of your hotel room door."

"I'll be right out." The line went dead.

Within seconds he joined her in the hall and shut the door behind him. His famous scowl was more pronounced than earlier in the day. "Saskia and I have been having problems, but I can't afford to end things with her until after the picture's finished. She doesn't know my intentions of course."

Dana was glad her father was coming to his senses for his own sake.

"She begged me to let her stay in the adjoining room while we work out our differences."

Poor Saskia. "That sounds reasonable."

His eyes darted to her suitcase. "Saskia's room is free at the hotel in Angers. I called and told the concierge to have it waiting for you."

"Thank you," she muttered, "but I'll make my own arrangements."

There was a long silence before he said, "If you go back to the château, you do so at your own peril."

Their gazes clashed. "And Monsieur Martin's, too?"

His eyes flashed with temper. "How did that man get his tentacles into you so fast?" he countered.

Dana stood her ground. "Why won't you answer the question, Dad?"

It took him forever to respond.

"I still forbid you, but as you reminded me earlier with all the carelessness of your culture, you're not seventeen anymore."

He went back in the bedroom. As she turned away, she heard the door close. Despite his hurtful remark, she was confident he wouldn't penalize Alex. Not because he'd had a sudden attack of human decency, but because he knew he'd never find a spot this perfect for his film.

Her throat felt tight all the way back to the château where she discovered the gate had been closed. A symbolic dagger for the trespasser to beware?

She closed her eyes, afraid she was being as superstitious as her father. After a minute, she reached for her purse and pulled out the remote. Once she'd driven on through, she shut it again, then continued on to the courtyard.

After getting out of the car, she tried to open

the front door, but it was locked and Alex's truck was nowhere in sight. He might still be around the back, working. Acting on that possibility, she drove to the other end of the château. It wound around to the orchard.

He wasn't there.

A hollow sensation crept through her. She checked her watch. It was already eight o'clock. Disturbed that he might have made plans with a woman and had gone into Angers for dinner, she drove to the front of the château once more.

Of course she could phone him, but he wouldn't appreciate a call if he was with someone else. Besides, he'd thought she'd gone back to the Hermitage for good. The only thing to do was drive to the next village in the opposite direction from Chanzeaux where she wouldn't run into her father by accident. After grabbing a bite to eat, she would come back and wait for Alex.

"*Bonsoir*, Monsieur Martan."

"*Bonsoir*, Madame Fournier. Has Mademoiselle Lofgren checked in yet?" He hadn't seen Dana's car outside.

She shook her head. "*Non, monsieur.* She doesn't have a reservation here."

"Then her father isn't staying here, either?"

"But of course he is! The person in the adjoining room is Mademoiselle Brusse. She's an actress doing a film with *le fameux* Monsieur Lofgren."

His hands clenched in reaction. If Dana hadn't come here, then she'd probably driven into Angers to get herself a hotel room. The last trip to the landfill had cost him time before he'd showered and changed clothes, thus the reason he'd missed her.

"Merci, madame." Before she could detain him with more gossip, he went back outside to phone Dana from the truck. It rang seven times. He was about ready to hang up in frustration when he heard her voice.

"Alex?" She sounded out of breath.

"What's wrong?" he demanded without preamble.

"My left front tire is flat. I've been trying to work the jack, but I've been having problems. Pretty soon I'll figure it out."

The band constricting his lungs tightened. "Where are you exactly?"

"Somewhere on the road between Rablay and Beaulieu."

"I'm on my way." He started the engine and

drove away from the hotel. "Stay in your car and lock the doors."

"Don't worry about me."

"What caused you to go in that direction?"

"When you weren't at the château, I decided to get dinner in the next village, but I never made it."

The blood hammered in his ears. "You came by the château?"

"Yes. Dad and Saskia have been quarreling. It's nothing new, but while they work things out she's going to stay in the adjoining room."

"Why did you come back?"

"In order to ask if I could rerent my bedroom so to speak, that is if you don't mind."

He muttered something unintelligible under his breath.

"What did you say, Alex? I'm not sure we have a good connection."

This had nothing to do with the connection. His hand tightened on the steering wheel. "And your father approves?"

There was a brief silence. "No. Does that mean there's no room at the inn?"

Ciel! "You know better than to ask that question." The fact was just beginning to sink in that she'd come to him whether her father liked it or not.

"You sound upset. In case I've ruined your plans for the evening, please forget about me. If I can't fix the tire, I'll walk to the château and wait until you come home later."

"No, you won't—" A woman who looked like her wasn't safe in daylight. Alex didn't even want to think about her being alone in the dark.

"I realize you think I'm too young to do anything on my own, but I'm not helpless."

"Age has nothing to do with it. I'm just being careful."

"Point taken," she admitted in a quiet voice.

His body relaxed. "Where would you like to eat tonight?"

"You mean you haven't had dinner, either?"

"As a matter of fact, I went to the Hermitage in the hope we could drive into Angers for a meal, but Madame Fournier informed me a certain actress had taken over your room."

"Saskia didn't waste any time announcing herself."

"Madame Fournier lives for such moments."

Her sigh came through the line, infiltrating his body. "I don't want to talk about either of them. I'm too hungry. To be honest my mouth has been watering for one of those quiches we bought in Angers. Are there any left?"

He smiled. "I've saved everything for us. There's more than plenty for several meals." Alex preferred dining in tonight where he didn't have to share her with anyone. While his thoughts were on their evening ahead, he saw her car at the side of the road and pulled off behind her. "Don't be alarmed. I've got your car in my headlights."

"I have to admit I'm glad it's you. I'll hang up."

Alex heard the slight quiver in her voice before the line went dead. Though he had no doubt she could handle herself in most situations, her relief was evident. So was his now that he'd caught up to her.

After shutting off the ignition, he reached in the glove box for his flashlight and got out of the truck. She rolled down the window and poked her beautiful golden head out the opening. He caught the flash of those startling blue eyes in the light.

"Did I do it wrong?"

For a second he was so concentrated on her, everything else went out of his mind. "Let me take a look," he murmured, before shining the light on the tire. It was flat, all right.

She climbed out of the car. "What can I do to help?"

Her flowery fragrance seduced him. "If you'll hold the flashlight right there, I'll have this changed in a minute."

Their fingers brushed in the transfer, increasing his awareness of the warm feminine body standing behind him. He hunkered down to work the jack and remove the tire. Several cars slowed down as they passed before moving on. "You must have picked up a nail."

"I'll get it fixed tomorrow." When he started to get up she asked, "Would you like the light to find the spare?"

"Thank you, but I don't need it."

He opened the car door to trip the trunk latch. Except for her sleeping bag, there was nothing else inside. That made it easy to retrieve the smaller tire and put it on. After he'd tightened the lug nuts, he lowered the car and put the flat in the trunk with the tools.

She walked toward him and handed him the flashlight. "You did that so fast I can't believe it."

"All it takes is practice. Over the years I've gotten a lot of it driving trucks out in areas where you have to do the repairs yourself or walk fifty miles."

"Thank you for coming to my rescue, even if you pretend it was nothing."

"It was my pleasure." Unable to help himself, he briefly kissed those lips that had been tantalizing him. They were soft and sweet beneath his. He wanted so much more, but not out here on the road in view of any passerby. "Now let's get back to the château. I'll follow you."

He helped her inside the car, then he jumped in the truck. She made a U-turn and headed for Rablay-Sur-Layon only a short distance off. Once they'd turned onto the private road, he pressed the remote so they could drive through the gate.

The noise it made clanking shut was the most satisfying sound he'd heard in a long time. It signaled that they'd left the world behind. For the rest of the night it was just the two of them.

CHAPTER FIVE

ALEX'S unexpected kiss had done a good job of melting her insides. She'd been wanting it to happen, but he'd caught her off guard out there on the road where other people could see them. To make things even more frustrating, he'd ended it too soon for her to respond the way she ached to do.

Dana had almost suffered a heart attack when she'd seen him walk toward her car dressed in a charcoal shirt and gray trousers. His rugged male beauty electrified her senses.

By the time he parked next to her in front of the château, she was feeling feverish with longings she couldn't seem to control. If she didn't get a grip, he'd be convinced he was dealing with a schoolgirl instead of a mature woman.

As she started to get out, he opened the back door and reached for her suitcase.

Being on her own so much, she had to

concede it was wonderful to be waited on and taken care of. When she looked back on the dilemma she'd been in before he'd phoned her, a shudder rocked her body. He'd spoken the truth. She wouldn't have been safe inside the car or walking back to the château alone.

Alex used his remote to open the front door. Once they were inside he put down her suitcase and turned on the lights. She felt his dark-eyed gaze rest on her. "Food before anything else, I think."

"I like the way you think."

By tacit agreement she followed him through the foyer past the staircase to a hallway leading to the west wing. He turned on another light. Dana hadn't been in this part of the château before. They passed a set of double doors.

"May I see inside?"

"Of course." Alex opened them for her. "This is a drawing room that opens into the grand dining room. As you can see, boards have been nailed over the broken windows. When they're repaired, they'll look out on the front courtyard."

The beauty of the interior caused her to cross her arms over her chest and rub her hands against them in reaction. "I've never seen anything so lovely. The ornate walls and ceilings make me feel like I'm in a palace. After this, you wonder how your mother adapted to life in a normal house."

"I'm sure my father did his share of worrying about it, but they had a good marriage which hopefully made up for a lot of things." Just then he sounded far away.

"Believe it or not, my parents had a solid marriage, too, albeit an unorthodox one. Mom had to make most of the concessions, but she must have wanted to, otherwise she would have left him because he's quite impossible."

Dana followed his low chuckle back out to the hall and down to a turn that opened up to the kitchen.

"How incredible!" It was massive with a vaulted ceiling and an open hearth fireplace that took up one wall. Modern appliances had been mixed in with the ancient. A long rectory-type table with benches sat in the middle of the room. She estimated sixteen people could be seated there comfortably.

"Through that far door on the right are the steps leading down to the wine cellar. The door at the other end of the kitchen leads to a pantry and an outside door. Another leads to a bathroom."

"You've reminded me I need to wash my hands after ineptly handling that jack. Excuse me for a moment."

She darted through the pantry stocked with supplies. A new washer and dryer had been installed in there. The pantry was big enough to be a master bedroom. Beyond it she found the bathroom Alex had upgraded. It wasn't quite as large as the one upstairs, but it had every accoutrement.

The tiles covering the walls and ceiling were the same as the ones lining the counters in the kitchen. Each was an original and had been hand-painted on a cream background to depict grapes, apples, pears, all the fruits probably grown on the estate.

Continually charmed by everything she saw, Dana was in a daze when she returned to the kitchen. She'd been gone so long, Alex had already put their meal on the table. He was standing next to one end with a bottle of wine in his hand.

"Sorry I got detained, but the tiles were so adorable I had to study them."

"Now that I'm getting to know you better, I find that entirely understandable. Sit down and I'll serve you." As she took her place, he uncorked it and poured the pale gold liquid into their glasses.

Their eyes met. "Is this a special wine?"

"It is now." His deep voice sounded more like a purr. He sat down opposite her and lifted his glass. "To us. May our unexpected month together hold many more pleasant surprises."

He'd just laid down the ground rules. She wasn't to read more into that kiss than he'd intended. After the month was over, this season of enchantment would come to an end. She smiled through her distress at the thought and clinked her glass against his. "To you, *monsieur*. May you outlive any regrets for your magnanimity."

With her emotions in turmoil, she forgot and drank her wine like it was water. Too late she realized her mistake and tried to recover without him noticing, but it wasn't possible considering she was choking. His dark brown eyes smiled while he munched on a croissant. "When you're able to speak again, tell me how you find your wine."

Embarrassed, Dana cleared her throat. "It's sweet like the one we had the other night, but it's not the same domaine, is it? This time I tasted honey."

"That's very discerning of you. When you seemed to enjoy the one we had at the Hermitage, I bought this bottle for you to try. It's another Layon wine called Chaume from the Domaine des Forges. I'm told it's the sweetest of all."

She got this fluttery feeling in her chest. Anxious not to appear disturbed by him, she bit into the quiche he'd warmed for them. It wasn't just his words, but the way he said them. Here she'd promised herself not to get carried away, but being alone with him like this caused her to think many forbidden thoughts.

"You were very thoughtful to do that. Now that I've sampled both, it makes me wonder what the Belles Fleurs wine tasted like."

"We'll never know…" His voice trailed. "Every bottle has disappeared from the wine cellar. I suppose there are a few connoisseurs who bought them up. They might still have them stored in their wine cellars for a special occasion. Good dessert wines can last for decades."

"It seems so sad there's no more wine being made from the grapes grown on your property."

He stared at her, deep in concentration. "I'm afraid I'm not a vintner. It's a whole other world that requires the best oenologist you can hire.

A wine expert doesn't come cheap, nor a vintner and crew."

"What do you suppose happened to the records kept by the vintners of this estate?"

"I have no idea. Possibly they're hiding in one of the tons of boxes holding the contents of the library. You haven't seen that room yet. It's in the right wing next to the music room."

After she finished off her quiche, she asked, "Are the books upstairs with the furniture?"

"They're in one of the third floor turret rounds."

She peeled an orange and ate several sections as she digested what he'd told her. "Alex—aren't you curious about them? About the history of this place?"

He ate some cheese before swallowing the rest of his wine. "Not particularly."

"Why?" When he didn't immediately answer her, she felt terrible. It was clear he didn't want to talk about his family's past. "I'm sorry. I didn't mean to pry. It's none of my business."

Unable to sit there any longer, she jumped up and started clearing the table.

"Leave it, Dana."

Ignoring his edict, she took everything over to the sink. "I want to make myself useful before I go upstairs."

"You're tired then?"

"Yes." She seized on the opening he'd given her. "You must be, too, considering how early you get up and the exhausting labor you do every day." She found detergent to wash their plates and glasses.

Her heart skipped a beat when he joined her with a towel to dry them. Soon she had the table wiped off and the kitchen cleaned up. They were both standing at the counter.

"Since one of your jobs is to provide your father with his daily lunch, feel free to fix it here."

Surprised by the offer, she lifted her head to look at him. "I would never presume on your generosity like that. I've already made arrangements with the Hermitage to bring them here. When everyone else breaks for lunch, he likes to stay put and eat alone. I always bring him hotel food when we're on location."

He stared at her through veiled eyes. "When I have a perfectly functional kitchen, that's a lot of needless going back and forth."

Dana's attraction to him was eating her alive. "I couldn't."

"Not even if I asked you to make lunch for me at the same time?"

Her heart skidded all over the place. "You

mean, and bring it out to you while you're working?"

Something flickered in the dark recesses of his eyes. "It would save me a lot of time and trouble."

Yes, she could see how a cook would make his life easier so he could get on with his business. In that regard he wasn't any different from her father.

"I have to admit doing something for you would make me feel a little better about staying on the premises."

"Good," he said in a voice of satisfaction. "I'm anxious to clear out the debris from the rest of the orchard as soon as possible."

"That's right," she murmured, trying to disguise her dismay. "You're in a hurry to leave for Louisiana." The thought of him not being on his property one day was anathema to her.

She rubbed her palms against her hips in a self-conscious gesture he took in with those dark, all-seeing eyes. "W-what do you like for lunch?" Her voice faltered.

He studied her for a moment. "I'm certain anything you make will be delicious."

His charm caused her breath to catch. "In the morning I'll do some grocery shopping when I go into Angers to get the tire repaired."

"As long as you're doing that, would you mind buying enough food to cover breakfast and dinner for a week, too? In the end it will save our energy for more important matters."

Except that her job of making sure her father had his lunch wasn't on the same scale of doing it for Alex. The thought was preposterous. "You trust me?"

"Let's just say I'm willing to go on faith."

Her lips curved upward. "That's very courageous of you."

Alex's eyes glimmered. "Just as long as you don't simmer pickled pigs feet in wine sauce and tell me it's chicken, we'll get along fine."

Her chuckle turned into laughter. She would love to freeze this moment with him. To be with a man like this, to be the recipient of his attention and enjoy his company in all the little private ways brought joy to her life she'd never experienced.

Early in the morning she'd take stock of his kitchen to find out what staples were on hand. While her mind was ticking off her plans, he pulled out his wallet and laid several large denominations of Eurodollars on the counter. Dana was too bemused by events to argue over who would pay.

"Merci, monsieur." After gathering them, she walked over to the bench where she'd been sitting and stashed them in her purse.

"De rien, mademoiselle." When he spoke French his whole demeanor changed, making her wholly aware of the sensual side of his nature. "Let me get some more candles and my flashlight from the pantry and I'll accompany you upstairs. You look sleepy."

As he walked off, she reflected on his words. A woman wanted to hear certain things from the man she found desirable, but *sleepy* relegated her to daddy's little girl status.

Since meeting him she had to concede he'd been protective of her. However, that didn't translate into a *grande passion* on his part. Though he'd brushed his lips against hers earlier, not by any stretch of the imagination would she have called it hunger unbridled or anything close.

Afraid she was already giving off needy vibes, she left the kitchen ahead of him and walked through the château to the foyer. Eyeing her suitcase, she grabbed it and started up the stairs. He caught up to her at the top where there was no more light and guided her down the corridor to her room.

It wasn't really her room, but it's the way she thought of it. When the flashlight illuminated the interior, she felt she'd come home. The sensation stayed with her while he lighted fresh candles in the floor candelabra.

Avoiding his eyes, she put her suitcase down. "You didn't have to do that. My flashlight is right here next to the bed."

"I wanted to," came the deep velvet voice that was starting to haunt her. "Candlelight brings out the pink and cream porcelain of your skin. I've never met a woman with a complexion like yours."

What was she supposed to say to that? "Lots of people have told me I look like a cherub and pat me on the head."

His gaze narrowed on her mouth. "Don't you know any flesh and blood man seeing you doesn't dare do anything else for fear a bolt of lightning will strike him? Get a good sleep."

After he disappeared, she stood there shaking like the ground under her feet during a California earthquake.

On her return from Angers the next day, Dana parked around the end of the château and carried the groceries and other purchases into the kitchen through the side entrance. She'd purposely unlocked it before leaving.

Her father liked to eat at twelve-thirty sharp. She checked her watch. It was almost that time now. She hurriedly put things away, then made both lunches and packed them in the two baskets with a thermos of hot coffee each.

As soon as everything was ready she went in search of her father. He was in the grand salon opposite Alex's office talking with the two leads. In no time at all the staff had brought down furniture and everything was starting to take shape. Under Paul's watchful eye the place had become a beehive of organized commotion.

Knowing better than to disturb her dad, she stepped inside the room and put the basket next to the door. He didn't even glance at her before she darted back to the kitchen. Now she was free to deliver the second basket to the unforgettable male responsible for last night's insomnia.

Once she entered the orchard, the sound of sawing reached her ears. Alex had put the ladder against a different tree this time. Slowly but surely he was making progress. She admired him so much for doing everything single-handedly, she wanted to shout to the world how remarkable he was.

It seemed a shame he had to come down out of the tree for his lunch. Adrenaline gushed through her veins at the idea of taking it up to him. Why not? There was so much foliage, he could find a spot to secure the basket while he ate.

Without hesitation she started up the rungs, excited to repay him any way she could for his generosity. Almost to the top she called to him. "Alex?"

The sawing stopped. "Dana?" He sounded shocked. Evidently he hadn't seen her. "Where are you?"

Two more steps and she poked her head through the leaves. "Right here. The mountain decided to come to Mohammed," she quipped, but she didn't get the reaction she'd hoped for. His eyes pierced hers in fury.

In an instant his expression had grown fierce. Lines deepened around his hard mouth, giving him a forbidding expression. "Whatever possessed you to climb all the way up here? If you fell from this height, you could break a great deal more than your lovely neck."

She'd been prepared for a lot of things, but not his anger. "You're right. It was foolish of me. I didn't stop to think how guilty you would feel if anything happened to me and you'd be forced to report it to my father. *My* mistake. Here's your lunch." She formed a nest of leaves and propped it as securely as she could in front of him. *"Bon appetit."*

"Dana—" he ground out, but she ignored him. Without any encumbrance she was able to go back down the ladder in record time. He called to her again, this time in frustration.

"Stop worrying, Alex. You had every right to be angry!" she shouted back before running around the side of the château.

Since the rest of her day was free, she would go sightseeing. After grabbing her purse from the pantry, she made sure the door was locked, then got in her car and backed around to the front.

Her heart didn't resume its normal beat until she'd driven a good fifty kilometers on the repaired tire. At the next village she pulled off the road into a park. In the distance she saw some swans on a lake. The serene scene mocked the turmoil going on inside of her.

After the experience with Neal she'd promised herself she wouldn't get close enough to a man again to expose her deepest feelings. But the pathetic little stunt she'd just pulled revealed holes in her best intentions, forcing her to come face-to-face with her own idiocy.

The need to channel her roiling emotions drove her from the car. She spent the rest of the afternoon walking around the lake, making plans that had nothing to do with Alex. On the way back to the château she stopped for a meal and didn't return to Rablay until five-thirty.

She was relieved no one had gone to their hotels yet. With everyone still around, Alex would make himself scarce. That gave her time to reach her room without him noticing. She'd hibernate there until tomorrow. New day, new beginning.

No sooner had she started down the upstairs hall than she saw Saskia coming out of her bedroom. The brown-haired model turned actress could turn any man's head, but she didn't have the same effect on Dana. The invasion of privacy infuriated her under any circumstances, but if she'd been snooping around on orders from Dana's father, she was ready to declare war.

"Hi!" Saskia was a cool customer. She didn't have the grace to blush or act embarrassed. Dana couldn't bring herself to reciprocate with a greeting. "What did you have to do for the owner of this fabulous estate to give you special privileges?"

"Why don't you ask him yourself?"

"I haven't met him yet, but the girls in makeup tell me he's beyond gorgeous."

That was one way of describing him. Saskia's jaw would drop when she saw Alex for the first time. "Didn't Paul tell you the petit salon and this bedroom were off-limits?"

"I didn't think he meant me."

"Why not?"

Throwing back another question managed to unsettle her a little. "Actually I was looking for you in the hope we could talk."

"About what?"

"Now you're being obtuse. You know very well your father and I aren't getting along right now. I was hoping you'd be able to tell me what I'm doing wrong."

"I can't fault you for anything, Saskia. I wouldn't presume."

"That's no help."

Dana took a steadying breath. "That's because there is no answer. You're not my mother, but you've always known that, so the truth couldn't be a surprise to you. If it's any consolation, I can't do it right, either."

Saskia flashed her a shrewd regard. "Maybe if I stayed here at the château, Jan would worry about me sometimes? See me in a different light?"

You mean, as mistress of the manor with a real live Frenchman attached? Now things were beginning to make sense. She'd been looking for Alex…

"I'm sure I don't know."

"Do you think the owner of the château would let me stay here?"

"Haven't a clue."

She pursed her lips. "I suppose it helped that you're Jan's daughter. Maybe being his girl-friend would work for me."

"It's worth a try."

Her green eyes gleamed in anticipation of confronting Alex. "I agree. Thanks for the talk."

Dana watched her slender figure disappear before she went to her bedroom. Saskia had been fighting a losing battle when it came to Dana's father. No doubt seeing the eight-by-ten photograph of Dana's mother and a smaller photograph of her parents propped on the dresser underlined the futility of Saskia's relationship with him.

As for Dana, she had her own problem in the futility department where Alex was concerned. He couldn't leave for the States fast enough. How ironic that because she'd seen his ad on the Internet, she'd unwittingly made it possible for him to reach his goal sooner. Saskia could dream all she wanted, but she was in for a shock.

Alex worked in the orchard until twilight. One more trip to the landfill and he'd call it a night. The delicious, filling lunch Dana had delivered air express without consideration for her personal safety had kept him going through the dinner hour.

Much as he'd wanted to go after her, he hadn't wanted an audience that included her father, *grace a dieu*. Since no one knew what had transpired, he decided it would be better to apologize to her after hours when they were alone.

On the way back from his last haul, he locked the gate for the night and drove on to the front of the château. The sight of her rental car meant she was home. His pulse shot off the charts as he hurried inside and made a quick inspection of the ground floor in the hope he might bump into her.

To his chagrin all he found besides furniture in the grand salon was an empty basket and thermos placed at the foot of the paneled door. It was identical to the one she'd brought Alex. He carried it to the kitchen where he'd put his on the way in from the truck.

A few minutes later after a shower and

change of clothes, he phoned her while he was warming some food for his dinner. Maybe she'd come down and join him.

"Alex?" She answered on the fourth ring. "Is there something wrong?"

"Yes," he blurted. At this point in their relationship, nothing but honesty would do.

"Did you lose your remote and can't get in the château?"

"I'm afraid my problem can't be fixed that easily."

He felt her hesitate before she said, "Did the studio from Paris cancel on you for mid-September?"

The strong hint of anxiety in her tone plus the fact that she remembered what he'd told her humbled him. He'd grovel if necessary to get back on the footing they'd had before she'd brought him his lunch.

Alex cleared his throat. "I appreciate your concern, but the truth is, I was rude to you earlier today. It takes a lot to frighten me, but when I saw you appear among the leaves like some impossibly adorable wood nymph and realized how far you were from the ground, I lost any perspective I should've had."

She let out a wry laugh. "The relegation from

cherub to wood nymph is a subtle improvement I like, so I'll take it."

Dana...

"As for the rest, I've had all day to ponder my actions over that brainless stunt. Chalk it up to the enchantment of this place."

He had to clamp down hard on his emotions. "I can safely say it was the best meal I ever had in a tree."

"That's another distinction I'll treasure, but to save you from an early heart attack, I'll leave your lunch basket on the fender of your truck from now on."

"Why don't you come downstairs and we'll talk about it over a glass of wine." If he hadn't made the rule that he would never take advantage by going up to her room after dark unless invited, he'd be there now.

"Lovely as that sounds, I'm already half asleep. May I confess something to you?"

"By all means." He had to swallow his disappointment.

"You'll think me more superstitious than my father."

That particular word wasn't on the growing list of adjectives he found himself ascribing to her. The mention of her father in the same conversation didn't improve his mood. "Don't keep me in suspense."

"Somehow it seems sacrilegious to drink anyone else's wine on Belles Fleurs property. Does that make sense?"

His eyes closed tightly for a minute because deep in his core he'd had the same thought last night. Like the seed of the precious *chenin blanc* grape buried in the soil of the Anjou centuries ago, it seemed to have germinated out of nowhere, reminding him of his mother's roots.

"More than you know," he answered huskily.

Until last night he hadn't felt that emotional connection. Now, suddenly, it tugged at him and he realized it was all tied up with Dana, who had everything to do with this unexpected awakening.

"Alex? Are you still there?"

"Mais oui." He gripped the phone tighter. "Do you remember asking if I could see the famous Belles Fleurs vineyard from the top of the tree?"

"Are we talking about the same question you didn't answer?"

"Meet me out in back in the morning at eight. There's something I want to show you."

"I thought I'd been warned off climbing trees."

Alex rubbed the back of his neck absently. "This requires some walking. Wear boots if you have them."

"I don't. Will trainers do?"

"Those will protect your feet better than your sandals."

"We're not going to be trekking through some snake-infested region are we? I have an irrational terror of them."

A low chuckle rumbled out of him. "Few of the snakes in France are venomous. Even then their bites aren't worse than wasp stings. So far I haven't come across any."

"That's not exactly reassuring, Alex."

"I've survived the snake worlds of Indonesia and Africa."

"But you're—"

"Yes?" he prodded after she broke off talking midsentence. She'd left him hanging, the perpetual state he'd been in since meeting her…and didn't like.

"I was just going to say you're invincible."

"Not quite." She'd been making inroads on his psyche from the moment they'd met, infiltrating his thoughts. No woman he'd known could claim that distinction. "For what it's worth, I promise to protect you."

"Thank you."

He wanted to be with her now. "Are you sure you're too tired for Scrabble? I brought the game with me from Bali. My father and I often played."

"In how many languages?"

He couldn't suppress his laughter. "Why don't we find out?"

"Maybe another night when I'm not worn-out."

"What's your birthdate?" She'd be turning twenty-seven. That wasn't a day he was bound to forget, not after his assumption that she'd been much younger.

"The sixteenth."

"Next Monday. Don't make any plans. We'll celebrate and I'll let you beat me."

"I intend to."

He grinned. "Where did you go today?"

"I don't really know. I kept driving until I saw this park and a lake. There was a mother swan. She had three cygnets who followed her around, matching her exact movements like they had radar. I kept running around the lake, watching them. You've never seen anything so sweet or fascinating."

Yes, he had... The picture he had in his mind of her made his whole body ache.

"No wonder you're tired. If you'd rather make it nine o'clock—"

"I'll probably be out there by seven-thirty before any of the crew arrives. I don't like them knowing my business."

Did that include her father? Alex had the strong hunch there'd been little communication between them by phone since she'd chosen to sleep at the château against his wishes.

"That's understandable."

"To be honest, I don't see how you can stand to have your own privacy invaded by a ton of strangers wreaking havoc."

He drew in a sharp breath. "It's called money."

"I know. Let's hope word has spread throughout the film world and you're flooded with new requests. Nothing would make me happier for you. Good night." The definitive click cut off his lifeline.

While he locked up and turned out lights, it came to him Dana was a gift that might come along once in a millennium *if* you were lucky. Her father had to know that. Perhaps it was the reason he guarded his golden-haired offspring so jealously.

In a very short period of time Dana had brought out the possessive instinct in Alex. Evidently it had been lying dormant these many years just waiting to spring to life when or if the right person ever made an appearance.

For the rest of the night he was taunted by dreams of a certain blue-eyed wood nymph smiling at him through the foliage. If the handsaw and the basket hadn't been in the way, the two of them might still be up there in a bed of leaves while he made love to her over and over again.

CHAPTER SIX

"SALUT, ma belle!"

She waved to Alex, who stood by the truck, dressed in thigh-molding jeans and another white T-shirt that revealed the outline of his cut physique. The sun brought out the black-brown vibrancy of his overly long hair, a style that suited him to perfection.

He'd seen her coming around the back in her white-washed jeans and T-shirt in her favorite mocha color. His eyes followed her progress with disturbing intensity, making her feel exposed.

"It's such a beautiful morning I'm not going to ask if you're fine because you couldn't be anything else." He was freshly shaven and the faint scent of the soap he'd used in the shower permeated the air around them.

"You're right about that," he murmured. She watched him pick up a pair of long-handled pruning shears. "Shall we be off?"

There was a slight curve to his lips she'd only tasted for a brief moment the other night. Unfortunately it had set up a permanent hunger nothing but a much longer repeat of the experience would satisfy.

Dana nodded before following him down the path that bisected the orchard. Maybe she was crazy but she felt something crackling in the air between them, the kind of thing that sizzled during a lightning storm.

He kept walking until they reached the perimeter of the orchard. Juxtaposed was a forest of briars taller than they were. It reached to the river, filling the entire hillside and around the bend. She'd never seen the likes of such a thing before.

A gasp escaped her lips. "The only thing I can compare this to are the briars that overgrew Sleeping Beauty's castle, but that was in a storybook."

He slanted her a mysterious glance. "If you recall, it was a *French* fairy tale." He folded his arms. "Behold the Belles Fleurs vineyard."

"No—"

As she tried to take it all in, her eyes smarted. She turned her head so Alex wouldn't see how it had affected her. Now she understood why he hadn't wanted to talk about it.

"This is what happens after eighty years of neglect," came his gravelly voice.

She shook her head. "When you drive here from Paris and see the rows of gorgeous green vineyards...to think they can look like this..." It was impossible to articulate her horror.

"Oh, Alex—for your family to let all of this die—it's beyond my comprehension." She wheeled around to face him. "How did you bear it when you saw this desecration?"

He put down the shears. "Don't be too sad." Taking a step toward her he wiped one lone tear from her hot cheek with the pad of his thumb. As their gazes fused, his hands cupped the sides of her face. "Believe it or not this vineyard is alive."

"But it couldn't be!"

"I assure you it is. Deep in those trunks are the makings of *chenin blanc* grapes grown on Belles Fleurs *terroir*."

"I—I can't fathom it."

"Vines are unusual creatures. They want to climb. They climb and they climb while the birds eat the fruit and drop the seeds where they will. What you're looking at is a tangled mess of what is probably the best prepared soil along the Layon. Eighty years lying fallow has made it rich. All the vineyard needs is a little work."

"A little—" she cried.

Chuckling quietly, he removed his hands and reached for the shears again, leaving her dizzy with unassuaged longings. "It would take five years to turn this into a thriving business again. The first year all these trunks would have to be cut down to three feet, like this."

She watched him in wonder and fascination as he shaped it down to size like Michelangelo bringing a figure out of the marble. He threw the castoff briars to the side. Dana crouched down to examine one of them. She lifted her head. "Then what happens?"

"The next year new canes appear." He tossed out another vine. Painstaking work. "They have to be treated like newborn babies."

When she smiled, he smiled back, giving her a heart attack. "You said five years."

He nodded his dark head. "In the third year you'd see buds. In the fourth, the first new grapes would appear. By the fifth year they'd be worthy of making a good wine."

"Five years…" He wouldn't be here in five years. The thought sickened her and she jumped to her feet. "When I asked you why you weren't concerned about the vineyard, it's clear why you chose not to answer me until now. They say a picture is worth a thousand words. In this case it's more like a billion."

"Vineyards are a business and family concern. Without one, or one that can't pull together, it doesn't warrant the effort it takes to make wine." There was a residue element in his voice, maybe sadness. It brought a lump to her throat.

"No. I can see that..." Her voice trailed. "Does this mean you're considering leasing the vineyard or even selling it to a prospective vintner?"

"I'm not sure." They started walking back. She could tell he was eager to get busy in the orchard. It was time to change the subject.

"Alex? You know what a bookworm I am. Would you consider it a horrible invasion of your privacy if I went through some of the boxes in storage, just to see what was in the library? I don't speak French, but I can read enough to understand titles and that sort of thing."

"Be my guest."

Excitement welled inside her. Maybe she'd find some family records or scrapbooks he would enjoy looking at. "You mean it?"

His dark eyes seemed to be searching her very soul. "What do you think?"

"Thank you!" she cried. Without conscious

thought she put her hands on his upper arms and raised up on the tips of her sneakers to kiss his jaw. What happened next happened so quickly, she never saw it coming. Alex dropped the shears and crushed her against him, covering her mouth with his own.

She didn't know who was hungrier. All that mattered was that he was kissing her until she felt pleasure pains run through her body clear to her palms. Though she knew she couldn't die from rapture, she felt she was on the verge.

When she moaned, he whispered, "My sentiments exactly. Your mouth tastes sweeter than any Anjou wine in existence."

"Alex—" Her body shook with needs bursting out of control. She circled his neck with her arms in order to get closer and pressed little kisses along his jaw. While Dana couldn't get enough of him, his hands splayed across her back, drawing her up against his chest where she felt the thud of his heart resound.

"You're so incredibly beautiful, Dana. Help me stop before I can't." His breathing sounded shallow.

She hushed his lips with a kiss. "I don't want to stop."

He groaned. "Neither do I, but someone's coming."

Thinking that whoever it was was ruining the moment, she had to force herself to leave his arms. Still breathless from their passion, she turned in time to see Saskia in the distance. She walked toward them with purpose.

Of course. Who else.

"Well, hello," Saskia said on her approach, eyeing Alex in stunned surprise that any man could be that attractive. At thirty years of age, Saskia looked good herself and knew it. She eventually tore her eyes away to stare at Dana. They looked greener than usual. "Aren't you going to introduce us?"

"Saskia Brusse? Please meet Monsieur Alexandre Martin, the owner of the estate, Alex, Saskia is my father's girlfriend. She also happens to be one of the actresses in the film."

"But my part doesn't come until we're in Germany which is lucky for me."

"And what part is that?" Alex asked.

She blinked before staring at Dana. "You mean you haven't told him?"

Dana refused to be put off by her. "We haven't discussed the script."

Alex shook hands with her. "I'm happy to make your acquaintance, Mademoiselle Brusse."

"Thank you. You know, I was hoping to talk to you this morning. That's why I drove over here with Jan this early."

"Why did you want to see me?"

"Didn't Dana tell you about that, either?"

"I'm afraid we've had other matters on our minds. Please enlighten me."

While Dana willed her heart to stop racing, little red spots tinged Saskia's cheeks. She didn't like the way this conversation was going. "Jan told me Dana was staying here at the château. I wondered if I might occupy one of the rooms for the rest of the month, too. While we're here in France I have a lot of time on my hands and this is such a beautiful place."

"I'm glad you think so," Alex said with a smile. "But I don't allow anyone to live here with me except my staff. Dana is helping me put Belles Fleurs' library in order. It's quite a task. Since you're acquainted with her, then you're aware she's an historian like her father. Both are brilliant."

He picked up the shears. "Now, if you ladies will excuse me, I have to get to work. It was nice meeting you, Mademoiselle Brusse. When the film is out, I'll look forward to seeing it."

Dana had never seen anyone think on his feet that fast! Poor Saskia didn't know what had hit her. For that matter, neither did Dana... No man had ever shown her the respect or treated her the way Alex did. To defer to Dana and compliment her in front of Saskia was a new experience.

When another man might have let her sleep in the château using her sleeping bag, he'd gone out of his way to pamper her like a cherished guest. The night she'd had car trouble, he'd been there for her in an instant. He worried about her safety.

Alex was the antithesis of her father.

From the corner of her eye she noticed Saskia watching his hard-muscled body with a combination of anger at not having gotten her way and undisguised hunger. Suddenly she turned to Dana. "I saw you two before you saw me. Mixing business and pleasure can be risky."

"As you've found out with Dad," Dana drawled. "Given enough time we all live and learn. Talk to you later, Saskia." Without staying to listen to anything else, Dana hurried up the path and around to the side entrance of the château.

Alex was already up in a tree pretty much out of sight. Although he'd only claimed that Dana was working for him to checkmate Saskia, he'd given Dana permission to rummage through the boxes on the third floor. He was wonderful!

Because of his generosity, she was determined to find out anything she could about Belle Fleurs's history. Surely there'd come a day when Alex would want to know more. After she'd fixed the lunches, she'd go up and make an initial foray.

In the meantime she needed to keep working on his dinner for tonight. She wanted to cook him something authentically French. Yesterday she'd bought all the ingredients for it and had already done some preparations. On her way into the kitchen, she plucked her mother's French cookbook from the pantry shelf where she'd left it. She opened it to the desired page.

Soak an oxtail, cut in joints, in cold water for several hours.

"I've already done that."

Wipe with a clean cloth, and brown in butter with four onions and three carrots, coarsely chopped. When the meat is brown add two crushed cloves of garlic. Cover for two minutes, then add five tablespoons of brandy. Light this

*and let it burn for a moment, then add one half
bottle of dry white wine, and enough bouillon
so that the meat bathes in the liquid. Add salt,
pepper, a bouquet garni, and cook slowly for
three hours with the cover on.*

In a little while she had it cooking on the
stove. Next task.

*Saute in butter one half pound of mushrooms,
a good handful of diced fat bacon and about
one dozen small onions.*

She'd do that after she made the lunches and
delivered them.

Later on in the afternoon she checked the
recipe for more instructions.

*Add the meat to this and pour over all the
liquid which has been strained and from which
the fat has been removed. Cover and cook for
one hour more in a slow oven. The meat should
be soft and the sauce unctuous without recourse
to thickening with flour.*

During the hour it was cooking, she hurried
up the stairs. A few of the crew waved to her,
but no one wanted to talk. Her dad was somewhere around, but they didn't bump into each
other. That suited her just fine considering that
Alex had put Saskia's ski jump nose out of
joint. No doubt she'd already reported to Dana's

father what she'd seen in the orchard and had distorted it further.

Eager to explore, Dana took one of the side staircases to the third floor and walked the length of the château to the turret round. When she opened the door, all she saw was a sea of boxes in the musty room. Dozens and dozens of them. None were marked. Whoever had packed things up hadn't bothered to take the time to label anything. What a shame.

She tried opening a few, but she would need a knife or scissors to do the job. Some markers to identify what was in the boxes wouldn't hurt, either. And she'd need a chair. And some rags to clean off the dust. Tomorrow when she came up, she'd be prepared.

Once she'd returned to her bedroom, she put a change of clothes and some nightwear in a large bag she'd bought yesterday. It could hold most anything and was a lot easier to carry than a suitcase. A few toiletries and the contents of her purse and she was ready to go.

Dana stood at the top of the staircase and waited until no one was in the foyer, then she descended quickly and darted to the kitchen. It smelled good in here if she said so herself. In fact, it smelled the way a proper French kitchen should.

Pleased with her efforts, she turned off the oven, took the pot out and set it on one of the burners of the stove. With everything in order, she went over to the table and pulled out her notepad.

Monsieur Martin— Better put that in case anyone came in here and read it. *Your dinner is on top of the stove. All you have to do is heat it for a few minutes. Just so you know, I'll be staying in Angers overnight, but I promise I'll be back in the morning.*

D.

She put the note on the counter by the sink where he always washed his hands. That way he'd be sure to see it. With that accomplished she slipped out through the pantry to the side entrance and walked around the front of the château to her car.

Some of the cast and crew were getting in their vehicles. They all said hello to each other before she drove off. If Alex could see her leaving from his high perch in a treetop, so much the better.

After the way she'd responded to him in the orchard, she didn't want him thinking what he was entitled to think. Heat poured into her cheeks remembering how she'd practically devoured him. At eight o'clock in the morning no less!

Last night she'd practiced painful self-control and hadn't joined him when he'd phoned her. Tonight she knew she'd cave if he so much as looked at her. The only wise thing to do was remove herself from temptation in the hope of gaining some perspective. Since meeting Alex, she had absolutely none.

Dana must have brought Alex his lunch while he'd been sawing and couldn't see her. When he came down the ladder, there was the basket sitting on top of his truck. Though disappointed she hadn't called to him, he found himself salivating for his meal.

Tonight he intended to take her out for dinner and dancing. She couldn't plead fatigue two nights in a row! He needed her in his arms and wasn't going to let anything stand in his way.

Making it an early night, he did his last haul at six and slipped into the side entrance of the château with his basket, eager to find her. When he walked through the pantry to the kitchen, something smelled wonderful. His gaze went to a covered pot on the stove.

He set the basket on the counter and drew a fork from the drawer. Dana had cooked something that smelled sensational. He lifted the cover, unable to resist putting one of the pieces of beef in his mouth. It was kind of fatty and mild, but the stock was rich. He needed a spoon for it.

As he reached for one he saw a piece of paper lying near the sink. The note was short and sweet. He let out a curse. *Dana Lofgren—What are you trying to do to me?*

Before he exploded, he needed to calm down. If she thought she was going to hide from him tonight, she could forget it. He'd find her at one of the hotels Paul had lined up for everyone. After her scare on the road the other night, she wouldn't dare go anywhere else.

His eyes flew to the pot. Alex wasn't about to eat the rest of it without her. Forget dinner and dancing! He made a place for the pot in the fridge and left the kitchen.

By the time he'd showered and changed, the château had emptied. He locked up and left for Angers, driving his truck over the speed limit. This time he wouldn't forewarn her with a phone call. No more of that.

He stopped first at the Beau Rivage, but they had no listing for her. His frustration grew when the Chatelet could tell him nothing. By the time he approached the concierge at the Metropole, he was beginning to wonder if she'd checked in at another hotel altogether.

"*Bonsoir, monsieur.* My name is Monsieur Martin from the Belles Fleurs estate in Rablay."

"Ah…it's a pleasure to meet you. I understand the members of the Pyramid Film Company staying with us are shooting a film at your château."

"That's right, *monsieur*. It's very important that I speak to Mademoiselle Brusse. I understand she's in room 140."

"*Non, non.* The beautiful actress was staying in room 122, but she's no longer with us. Mademoiselle Lofgren, the director's daughter, is occupying that room now."

"You have no idea where Mademoiselle Brusse went?"

He leaned forward. In a low voice he said, "I believe with the director."

It seemed he and Madame Fournier had a lot in common. "You've been very helpful. *Merci, monsieur.*"

"*Pas de quoi.*"

Now that Alex knew where his fetching cook would be spending the night, he left the hotel to do a few errands.

Heat from a hot sun still lifted off the cobblestones. A summer night like this was meant for lovers, but he'd never been affected to such a degree before. He was aware of wants and needs growing beneath the surface. To feel emptiness and dissatisfaction with his life after a hard day's work was a new phenomenon for him.

His jaw hardened. After discovering Dana would be gone until tomorrow, the idea of spending the night alone at the château sounded insupportable. How was it she'd become so important to him in two weeks' time?

Before long she'd be off to Germany. And then what? Paul intimated she had plans to become a director.

Alex should never have insisted she stay. Knowing she was around day and night had him tied up in knots. Yet if he were honest with himself, he'd be just as nuts if she'd stayed at the Hermitage. No hiding place was too far for him to find her, and find her he would, father or no father.

He'd decided to give her until ten o'clock. It was five to now. After putting his purchases in the truck bed, he returned to the hotel. Mademoiselle Brusse's room was on the third floor at the end of the hall. This experience reminded him of musical chairs, a game he'd once played in elementary school. Tonight, however, the adults had decided to make it musical bedrooms minus the accompaniment.

"Dana?" he called to her as he knocked. "It's Alex. I know you're using this room, so it would be useless to pretend otherwise."

"Why would I do that?" came a familiar voice behind him. He swung around in surprise to see her coming toward him in the same clothes she'd had on that morning.

The humidity had brought a flush to her cheeks. Her hair had little golden curls with more spring when she walked. His fingers itched to play with them. She was clutching a carton in her arms. Her eyes questioned his without flickering. "If you wanted to talk to me, why didn't you phone?"

He sucked in his breath. "Would you have answered?"

"Of course."

Since he hadn't tried, he couldn't accuse her of lying. "Why didn't you tell me you planned to leave the estate tonight?"

"Didn't you get my note?" She could play the innocent better than anyone he knew. "I left it by the kitchen sink."

"I saw it," he clipped out. "I'm talking about this morning."

A tiny nerve throbbed at the base of her throat. "If you recall, we were…interrupted."

"My memory's perfect," he murmured, unable to look anywhere except her mouth. She'd started a fire with it at the vineyard. "What about at lunch when you came and went so fast I wasn't aware of it."

She averted her eyes. "I didn't make the decision to stay in town until later in the day."

He glanced at the carton. "What have you got there? You're holding it like it's a newborn baby."

The color in her cheeks intensified. "Actually it's something very old and priceless."

Alex couldn't imagine. "In that case let's take it home in my truck where it will be safe and we'll enjoy that delicious dinner you made. The aroma that filled the kitchen was mouthwatering."

Her startled gaze flew to his. "Then you haven't eaten it yet?" She sounded disappointed.

"I ate part of it, but when I realized you'd gone, I put the rest of it in the fridge for us. After the trouble you went to, I didn't want to eat all of it alone."

It frustrated him she still wasn't convinced. When he didn't seem to be getting anywhere with her, he tried a different tactic. "Why don't I hold the carton while you gather your things.

Tomorrow I'll drive you back for your car. I have to come in town again anyway on business."

She bit the underside of her lip, increasing his desire for her. Hopefully it was a sign she was weakening. "All right," she finally sighed the words, "but please don't drop it. I couldn't replace it for a long time."

That sounded cryptic. At this point he was consumed by curiosity.

"I promise I'll guard it with my life."

It could *be* your life, Alex.

With her heart hammering, Dana handed him the carton. A few minutes later she'd packed everything in her bag and they left the hotel. In truth she hadn't wanted to stay here at all and had dreaded returning to the sterile room after accomplishing her objective. For him to have shown up tonight thrilled her to her tiniest corpuscle.

When they reached the truck, she lowered her bag behind the cab, then took the carton from him while he opened the doors with the remote. "Let me hold it again until you climb inside."

Alex could be so sweet. When she was settled, he gave the carton back and carefully shut the door. After they left Angers he flicked her a penetrating glance. "Did you discover anything of interest when you were opening boxes today?"

"Without tools I couldn't see inside one of them and none are marked. It was very frustrating, but tomorrow's another day. How's your orchard going?"

"Thanks to those lunches, I've accomplished two more hours of work this week. At this rate I should be finished by the end of the next one."

The days were going by too fast. Dana was starting to panic. "What's your next project?"

"To tackle the undergrowth between the château and the winepress building."

Before long everything on the outside would be done. That left the interior. With his work ethic, he'd have the place ready for tourists in no time.

She felt his eyes travel over her. "What are you thinking about so hard?"

"All the work you've been doing without any help."

"It's the kind I like."

Dana admired him more than she could say. "You obviously love the outdoors."

"I've always needed my freedom."

Oh—she knew *that*. Alex had already defined the boundaries of their relationship to the month of August. How else had he managed to elude marriage all these years? Deep in thought she didn't realize they'd entered the estate until she heard the gate clank behind them. He drove around to the side entrance and turned off the engine.

When he got out of the cab and opened her door, he flicked her what looked like a mysterious smile. "I've been looking forward to a midnight supper with you. It appears tonight's the night."

She'd dreamed of such a night. "Aren't you tired after slaving out in the heat all day?"

"On the contrary, I feel energized." On that exciting note he used his remote to let her in the château and turn on lights. While she hurried through the pantry, he followed with her bag and some purchases of his own.

"Where do you think you're going in such a rush?" He'd taken the pot out of the fridge and placed it on the stove to heat.

"I thought I'd put this away first."

He eyed the carton. "It's dark upstairs. You might fall and break whatever it is you're guarding so jealously."

Dana couldn't afford for that to happen. "You're right." She put it down on the counter.

"Why don't you sit on the bench while I wait

on you. After slaving over our dinner, you deserve a rest."

"I'd rather help, but first I need to wash my hands." She walked to the sink where she saw the note she'd left. When she'd written it, she never dreamed Alex would have come looking for her to bring her back. Her pulse was off the charts.

His actions had to mean something, but she was a fool if she thought he wanted more than a few weeks pleasure with her under his roof. Like this morning when she'd succumbed so easily, she could do it again and that frightened her.

Dana had been the one to ask if she could stay at the château. If anything, she'd been the one to take advantage of Alex, not the other way around. Whatever happened from here on out, she would have to accept the consequences and live with them.

Soon the smell of the meat wafted past her nostrils. When she turned, she noticed he'd already set the table. Along with French bread and the bottle of the wine they'd enjoyed the other night, he'd added an old silver candelabra with new candles.

Once he'd lit them, he turned off the kitchen light, transforming the room into an incredibly intimate setting. His eyes beckoned her to come and sit. The gleam in those dark depths sent a tremor through her body.

She twisted her napkin nervously as he brought the contents of the pot to the table in a wonderful old round bowl with handles. After sitting down opposite her, he ladled a portion for both of them onto their plates. "Bon appetit."

Dana hoped it was good and took a first bite. To her surprise it didn't taste like anything she'd ever eaten before. She took another, but it needed something. Maybe a baguette would help.

Alex had already eaten most of his. "My compliments to the chef. Among your many talents you're a superb cook, Dana."

She put her spoon down. "No, I'm not."

He flashed her a curious glance. "Why do you say that?"

"Because it's awful. I—I wanted to make you something spectacular," she stammered. "It's not."

"What do you call it?"

"See?" Tears threatened. "Even *you* don't know what it is."

"Isn't it beef?"

"No."

"If you're trying to tell me this is pickled pigs feet, I'm surprised it's this delicious."

"Wrong animal."

One dark brow lifted, giving him a sardonic look. "Cow?"

"No."

"Horse?"

"No!"

"Frog's legs?"

She shook her head. "You'll never guess. I found the recipe in my mother's French cookbook I brought with me."

He cocked his head. "Then this could cover anything from brains to innards to tongues."

"This is more of an 'end' thing. The *marchand* at the *boucherie* told me it was a great delicacy," she confessed.

"An end thing…" She could hear his brilliant mind turning over the possibilities.

When nothing was forthcoming she said, "It's oxtail. How can the French eat it? I think it's disgusting!"

CHAPTER SEVEN

ALEX'S explosion of laughter echoed off the limestone walls. It was the deep male kind, so infectious her tears turned to laughter, too.

He reached for her hand and squeezed it. His touch shot warmth through her system. "I'm touched that you went to so much trouble for me."

"I should have fixed you something *I* love. Because you're the kind of man you are, you would never say anything to hurt my feelings, but even I can tell this would have to be an acquired taste. It's too mild and fatty, a terrible thing to serve a hungry man."

"Terrible," he teased. His gaze slid to hers. It was alive with emotion. "Let's have some wine with it."

"No—wait—"

Her cry resounded in the room, wiping his sensual smile away. "Why? What's wrong now?"

"Nothing. It's just that I bought us a special

surprise while I was in town. Since I didn't think I'd be seeing you before tomorrow evening, I hadn't planned on producing it yet, but under the circumstances I think now is the perfect time."

"Do I get to open it?" He looked and sounded like an excited schoolboy waiting to tear away the wrapping on his long-awaited birthday present.

She nodded. "But please be careful."

In a few swift strides he reached the counter. She got to her feet and moved closer to watch him. The carton encased an old green bottle of wine packed in straw. He drew it out to examine the magenta and cream label. She'd already had the privilege. In fact, she'd stared at it for a long time, hardly able to believe she'd been able to buy anything so precious.

His face paled. "Domaine Belles Fleurs Coteaux-du-Layon Cuvee D'Excellence, 1892, Anjou, France." As he spoke the words, he sounded like a man who'd gone into shock.

Suddenly his eyes shot to hers. They were on fire. "Where did you get this?" His voice trembled.

"I went to an impeccable source. Madame Fournier was able to put me in touch with Monsieur Honore Dumarre, a wealthy businessman and wine connoisseur living in Angers. He had three bottles of Domaine Belles Fleurs from different vintages in his wine cellar. When I explained why I wanted one, he was gracious enough to sell this to me."

She could see Alex's throat working. Even his hand was trembling. "A bottle like this can cost upward of five thousand dollars. Even meeting his full price, he'd have an almost impossible time parting with it."

Dana smiled. "Once in a while it helps that I'm Jan Lofgren's daughter. The fact that he's shooting his latest film on the Belles Fleurs estate went a long way to make up his mind for him. I threw in the fact that the new owner lived on the other side of the world until now and has never tasted his family's wine before."

Alex resembled a war victim suffering shell shock. "I have no words for what you've done," he whispered, "but you have to return it and get your money back."

She took a fortifying breath. "I knew you'd say that, but I did it for the pleasure it gave me. Do you know he wants to meet you? He'll be phoning you to make the arrangements."

Alex's face darkened with lines, revealing the remote quality she sometimes glimpsed, the quality that made her shiver. "Didn't you hear me, Dana? If you don't return it, I will." He'd already taken possession of the bottle and put it back in the carton. It sounded like he hadn't heard anything else she'd told him.

Her chin lifted defiantly. "That was *my* gift. It came from my own savings, not the studio's funds, in case you were worrying."

"If your father knew about this…"

At the mention of her dad, her anger was kindled. "Do you intend to tell him?" she fired. "Go ahead. But if you think blackmail will make me change my mind, then you don't know me at all."

"Dana," his voice grated. "This isn't the kind of thing you give someone."

"Well, pardon me, but I thought I just did. Some friends give cars—jewels—in the profession my father works in, I've seen it all. It pleased me to give you something of your mother's history, the only tangible evidence left of a thriving estate. Where's the romance in your soul?"

His hands knotted into fists. "We're talking about your hard-earned money."

She shrugged her shoulders. "There's money, and then there's money. I've never had anything

I wanted to spend it on before. But I should have remembered that you're in dire straits and need to get the taxes paid, so I tell you what. You go to Monsieur Dumarre. When you get the money back, you use it to make another installment to the bank so you can get out of here sooner and pursue your career."

Blind with pain, she grabbed her bag and flew down the long corridor to the foyer. She didn't need a light upstairs. Dana knew the place blindfolded. The second she reached her room, she threw herself on the bed.

"Dana—"

She might have known he'd be right behind her. Now she couldn't sob into the pillow. "Come back downstairs so we can talk."

"I'd rather not."

"Then I'm coming in. Just remember I gave you a choice."

When she heard the door open, she sat up on the bed and turned on the flashlight next to her bed. At first glance he looked ashen-faced, but maybe it was the starkness of the light against the dark.

Alex pulled the chair away from the writing table he'd provided earlier and sat down. He leaned forward with his hands clasped between his legs and stared at her for several tension-filled moments. "Your gift has over-whelmed me."

She lowered her eyes, too full of conflicted emotions to speak.

"Dana—how can I make you understand I've never known generosity like yours. I'm touched beyond my ability to express what I'm feeling."

His sincerity caused the tightness in her chest to break up. "I guess I wanted us to know what it tasted like so much, I went overboard in your opinion. But honestly, Alex, it wasn't that much money."

"How much?" he demanded quietly. "The truth."

"He gave me a discount as a welcome-to-Anjou gift for you. It only cost three thousand dollars. You see? Not as much as you'd imagined. It's less than what I make a month."

A sound of exasperation came out of him. She wanted to reach him, but how?

"Can't you understand how happy it made me to find a bottle of wine that came from *your* vineyard? After seeing the condition it's in now, it's like—I don't know—it's like finding this amazing treasure."

The torment on his handsome face killed

her. "There's only one way I'd accept it," his voice grated.

She jumped off the bed. "I won't let you pay me for it, so I'll keep it for my own souvenir from France. One day I'll open it for an important occasion a-and I'll remember," her voice faltered. "Now let's forget the whole thing, because I have." She started for the door.

"Where do you think you're going?" He was on his feet in an instant.

"Down to the kitchen to throw out the rest of that awful *Hochepot en boeuf*." Dana had to get out of there before she blurted what she really wanted to say—that she was in love with him, the gut-wrenching kind that went soul deep!

Her father would call it temporary madness, but he would have to be careful because this intensity of feeling had happened to her mother after meeting the enigmatic Swede. Her world had never been the same after that, either.

"The dishes will keep." Alex had caught up to her near the top of the stairs. He swept her in his strong arms like she was weightless and carried her back to the turret round.

"No, Alex—" she cried, trying to squirm out of his tight grasp. "Now you're feeling sorry for me like I'm a little girl who'll be all better with a peck on the cheek and a lollipop."

He laid her on the bed and followed her down so he half covered her with his hard-muscled body. She felt his fingers furrow into her hair, as if he loved the texture. "You don't have any comprehension of what I'm feeling. Would that you were a little girl I could send home to your daddy. But you're not," he muttered in what sounded like anguish.

"You're a big girl I'd like to keep locked up in this tower for my pleasure." His lips roved over her features, setting tiny fires. "Do you understand what I'm saying?"

Her heart leaped. "Then stop tormenting me and really kiss me. I've been in pain since this morning when Saskia interrupted us."

"I've been in pain much longer than that," he confessed.

The way his mouth closed over hers produced such ecstasy, she knew nothing except that this marvelous man was creating a vortex of desire deep within her. No other feeling in the world could compare. They gave kiss for kiss, savoring the taste and feel of each other. Divine sensations held her in thrall.

As time passed she needed to get closer and

slid her hands around the back of his head, luxu-riating in the freedom of touching and kissing him. He groaned against her tender throat. "You have no idea how much I want you."

The feel of their entwined bodies created heat, making her feverish. His caresses caused her breathing to grow shallow. "Alex—" she cried in a rapturous daze, clinging to him with helpless abandon.

"What's wrong?" he whispered against her swollen lips.

Wrong?

His hands stilled on her shoulders. "Am I frightening you? This is all too new to you, isn't it. Tell me the truth."

In that second while her mind was still capable of hearing him, she felt her heart plummet to her feet. Didn't Alex know she'd cried out his name in a state of euphoria?

The thought came to her that he would never have asked that question if he'd considered her his equal. That was because he didn't see her as a mature woman. It stunned her that his first impression of her still clung to him. In his eyes she was a girl disobeying her father's wishes—a girl so impulsive she thought nothing of sleeping in a château with a stranger and worse—spending $3,000 of her money on a whim.

Dana forgave him for that. Of course she did. She was also aware few men would have been as decent in this situation. But as long as he saw her in that light, it took away some of tonight's joy. Maybe no man would ever take her seriously if she continued to be associated with her father. Neal had been a case in point. Slowly she removed her arms from around his neck.

Tonight this unparalleled experience had given her a lot to think about. Though it killed her, she eased away from him. "You didn't frighten me, but I guess if we're being truthful, I am somewhat nervous that things have escalated so fast."

His handsome profile took on a chiseled cast before he got up off the bed. He stood at the end with his powerful legs slightly apart, away from the flashlight's beam. "I made a vow I'd never cross your threshold while you stayed here. Tonight I broke it, but I swear to you it will never happen again."

"Alex—there's no one to blame. We both lost our heads for a little while. It's human. I'd be lying if I didn't admit I enjoyed every minute of it, but as long as we're being honest, I wish you'd tell me something."

His shadowed eyes swept over her in intimate appraisal, waiting.

"Would you rather I left? Arrangements have already been made for me to stay in Saskia's room at the Metropole."

The way his mouth tightened into a thin line made her shiver. "That decision is entirely up to you. Meet me at the truck at seven-thirty in the morning and I'll drive you to Angers to get your car."

Her heart thudded till it hurt. By asking him that question, she'd proved she was the girl he'd called her, not a woman who acted on her own. Let it be the last mistake she made. "Thank you. Good night."

His dark eyes impaled hers before he disappeared out the door.

She sat on the bed for a long time pondering what to do. A girl would have a meltdown. A woman would brazen her way out of this.

He'd told Saskia that Dana was part of his staff; therefore she'd behave like an employee from here on out. She'd fix the lunches, but beyond that she'd leave him alone until she left the château. The man didn't have time for drama. He was in a hurry.

* * *

At six-thirty the next morning, Alex got up to fill the truck bed with debris. Might as well take another load to the landfill on the way to Angers. When he drove around the front of the château, his pulse sped up to find Dana waiting for him. She looked sensational in white pleated pants and a mini print top of blues and greens on a white background. He'd never known a woman so appealing, all golden and fresh as a piece of summer fruit.

"Good morning." She said it with such a friendly demeanor, last night's fireworks might never have happened. The minute she climbed in the cab, she brought the fragrance of strawberries with her, probably the result of her shampoo.

"You sound rested."

She opened her window. "I had a wonderful sleep."

His fingers tightened on the steering wheel as they headed for the gate. Throughout the endless night his desire for her had never cooled. He could still taste her mouth, feel the mold of her body. Though he'd told her it was her decision about staying or leaving, he hadn't meant it. The château wouldn't be the same without her in it. He'd made up his mind to do whatever was necessary to keep her sleeping on the premises.

"When I came down to the kitchen a few minutes ago, I couldn't find the wine bottle."

He flicked her a shuttered glance, feasting on her lovely profile. "I put it in the wine cellar for sakekeeping."

She flashed him an enticing smile. "That's where it should have been all along. Thank you."

Something was going on in that unpredictable brain of hers. Silence stretched between them. Before they left the landfill he said, "How would you like to tour Angers castle this morning? There won't be as many tourists this early. We'll escape the worst of the heat."

To his surprise she gave a caustic laugh that didn't settle well. "Do you know you're so much like my father at times, it's uncanny?"

His black brows met together in disbelief. "How did he get into this conversation?"

"When has he ever *not* been a part of it in some way or other? Last night you lit in to me. This morning you're trying to placate me. That has been his modus operandi since I was a child. Throw Dana a tidbit and she'll forget."

He gunned the engine and streaked out of there until they were beyond the view of any workers. Then he slammed on the brakes beneath the trees. Turning to her, he slid his arm along the back of the seat and encircled her warm nape with his hand. He could feel her pulse quicken beneath his fingers.

"I haven't forgotten one second of what happened last night and know in my gut you haven't, either." Unable to stop himself, he kissed her neck, knowing her skin smelled that sweet all over. "The fact is, I want you to stay at the château and was hoping to tell you that while we took a little time off to play. You were right about Jack being a dull boy."

"I wasn't planning to leave," she stated quietly, jolting him in that inimicable way of hers. "As for Jack, it's a well-known secret dull boys are usually the most successful because they never waiver from their goal."

Dana understood him so well, it hurt.

"Knowing how anxious you are to get the estate ready for the public, you won't be doing either of us a favor by taking me through that monster castle. I have my own plans for today. Thank you anyway."

The desire to drag her off to an undisclosed location and kiss her until she cried for mercy was trumped only by the knowledge that she wasn't going to run away from him yet. He bit her earlobe gently before separating himself from her so he could start up the engine.

Neither of them spoke for the rest of the drive into town. He didn't mind. For now it was enough to know she didn't want to leave the château. She loved everything about it including his damn grapes lying dormant inside those gnarled trunks.

It seemed the only drawback in the scenario was Alex.

"There's my car." Her voice jerked him from his torturous thoughts. He maneuvered his truck through the hectic morning traffic and pulled into a parking spot near hers.

She alighted before he could help her down. "You didn't need to get out," she told him as he followed her to the car.

"I'm the one who told you to leave it here overnight. Just looking to make sure everything works." He watched her get in, then shut the door for her. After checking the tires, he told her to pop the trunk. "Everything looks good."

She started the engine. "Thanks for driving me in. See you later." As she backed out and drove off, he waved until he couldn't see her golden head anymore. Turning sharply on his heel, he walked two blocks to the post office to collect his mail.

There were a few bills and letters from his colleagues in Bali, as well as his contacts in Louisiana. He would read them when he got back on the estate. As he finished cleaning out his mailbox, a postcard fell on the floor. He picked it up. The picture of Sanur gave away the name of the sender.

Martan—thank you for the postcard you sent with the big castle on it. One day I want to see it and the house your grandfather left you. I am working hard and am saving my money to come and visit. Maybe work for you one day in the States? Are the French women as hot as they say? How many have you had so far? Write soon, Sapto.

A smile broke out on Alex's face. He walked around the corner to a tourist shop where he bought a postcard with a photograph of the Château de Chenonceau, Dana's favorite. When he returned to the post office, he wrote a message on the back.

Hey, Sapto—I liked your card. It brought back many memories. I'm glad you're working so hard. It'll pay off. Maybe one day we'll see each other again. The French women are definitely hot, but they can't compare to the American woman staying at my château. I have plans for this one. Alex wrote the rest of his thoughts about her in Balinese and signed it, *A. Martin.*

After affixing a stamp, he mailed it, then left for home in his truck. Halfway to the estate it struck him that for the first time since being in France, he thought of it as home. Something was happening to him. Something profound.

Deep in thought about everything that had transpired last night, he almost didn't hear his cell phone in time to answer it. Hoping it was Dana, he almost said her name when he clicked on.

"Monsieur Martin?" a man asked in French. Disappointment swamped him.

"Oui?"

"This is Honore Dumarre. Perhaps Mademoiselle Lofgren hasn't had a chance to tell you about our meeting yesterday."

Alex straightened in his seat. Dana had warned him the other man would be calling, but he hadn't expected it this soon. "As a matter of fact, she presented me with an 1892 bottle of Belles Fleurs wine from your cellar last night."

The man chuckled. "Technically it wasn't from my wine cellar. I was just the keeper of it. Now I know why I held on to this one. It's a great honor for me to know it is now in the hands of the rightful owner. *Soyez le bien venu, monsieur.* I am so pleased to know a Fleury is back among us after all these years."

Something in Monsieur Dumarre's nature caused Alex to warm to him. "Thank you, *monsieur.* I'm touched by your words. As you can imagine, it was such an incredible gift, I'm still overcome. I'd intended to phone you before the day was out and thank you for parting with it."

"Mademoiselle Lofgren was so excited to give it to you, I couldn't have done anything else. Once in a while life offers us something beyond price. I'm not only thinking about the wine, but the beautiful young woman herself. Her soul shines right out of those heavenly blue eyes, doesn't it? What a prize she is."

"Yes," was all Alex could say because emotion had caught up to him.

"To think she's Jan Lofgren's daughter. His films are sheer genius."

"I agree."

"Did she tell you I'd like to host a party?" That was news. Dana probably would have told him if he'd given her half the chance. "All your vintner neighbors will want to meet you. I plan to invite the Lofgrens, too, and hope they can come."

"Thank you, Monsieur Dumarre. I'm sure it will please them to be included."

"*Excellent.* Call me Honore. My wife, Denise, and I were thinking Saturday, the twenty-eighth? Say seven o'clock? Would that be convenient?"

"I'll look forward to it with great pleasure. And please, call me Alex."

"*Bon.* It will be an evening everyone will look forward to."

"You're very kind."

"Not at all. *À bientôt,* Alex."

"*À la prochaine,* Honore."

On Monday morning Dana left the château early to meet with her father. She'd called him ahead of time to let him know she was coming. When she knocked on the hotel room door, he answered in his robe still drinking a cup of coffee.

"Hi, Dad." She moved inside, taking a glance around his messy room. "I'm here to run you to the hospital in Angers for your blood check. While I'm waiting for you, I'll do your wash with mine." She'd brought a laundry bag with her and started gathering up his things.

"I thought you'd forgotten."

How did he dare say that to her? It just proved

how unconscious he was where she was concerned. "Have I ever forgotten anything?"

He eyed her moodily. "I never see you." Oh, brother. "From what I understand you're too busy putting the library in order for Alex."

"I never see you, either." She turned it back on him. "You're so busy directing, the only way I know you've been at the château is to find the empty basket by the door to the grand salon every afternoon."

After a brief silence he said, "Your lunches are appreciated. You cook like your mother." He set the empty coffee cup on the table.

Dana almost dropped the load of clothes she was fitting in the bag. A compliment from him came around about as often as Halley's Comet. "She was the best."

"I miss her, too. Dana—will you sit down? I want to talk to you."

"Why?" She sensed a lecture coming on, his only reason for a talk these days.

"Because I want to give my daughter a birthday kiss. When you're in constant motion, I can't." He put his arms around her and hugged her hard. Emotion welled up inside her. She hugged him back.

"I thought you'd forgotten."

"I could hardly do that now, could I." With a kiss on her forehead, he let her go and pulled a familiar-looking bracelet out of his pocket. It was twisted like fine gold rope, very elegant, very chic. He fastened it around her wrist. "I gave this to your mother on her birthday before she died. Now I want you to have it."

For him to part with something of her mom's was unprecedented. "Thank you," she whispered. "Mother treasured this. I will, too."

"I know." He cleared his throat. "After the hospital, how would you like to spend the day with me? We'll do whatever you want to do and enjoy a meal at some unique restaurant."

Since she'd walked in the room, she'd sensed he had an agenda, but this offer was way too out of character for him. "What about Saskia?"

He frowned. "She's not invited."

"Can you leave your filming that long?"

"They'll get by without me for a day."

No, they won't! "I thought you were on such a rushed time schedule, you couldn't let anything interrupt the shooting of the film. Come on, Dad. Tell me the real reason."

His face clouded. "You need guidance."

"In other words you were going to spend my birthday giving me another lecture!"

"Is it true you purchased a bottle of Belles Fleurs wine for Alex from a Monsieur Honore Dumarre at a cost of $3,000?"

Dana felt like he'd just thrown a pickaxe at her heart. Had Alex betrayed her? She couldn't bear it.

"Yes."

"Yesterday I received a call from him. He invited me to attend a vintner party in honor of Monsieur Martin on the twenty-eighth and asked me to bring my lovely daughter, Mademoiselle Lofgren, with me. He was quick to remind me that true beauty and generosity like yours was rare in this world."

Relief that it wasn't Alex who'd told her father what she'd done filled her with exquisite relief. "How did he get in touch with you?"

"Apparently Madame Fournier at the front desk put you in touch with him in the first place. When he rang the hotel, asking for me, she put him through to my room."

"I see."

"Dana—don't you know Alex Martin is using you?"

Her father would never understand a man like Alex. He was a breed apart from anyone else. "I'm sorry you see it that way."

"Saskia saw you with him in the orchard the other day. From what she told me, I have every reason to be worried about you."

Saskia was furious that Alex hadn't given her the time of day, but her father couldn't see through it. He really was lost without her mother.

"You know what, Dad? It isn't good for us to be working together anymore. I love you very much, but after we're through here in France, I'm going back to California. I want to get myself an apartment and look for a job that can turn into a career."

She picked up the laundry bag. "Shall I wait for you in my car?"

He shook his head. "I'll drive myself to the hospital."

"All right. I'll get a key from the front desk so I can put your clean clothes in the room later. Thank you again for the gift. It's priceless to me."

Two hours later she'd finished all her errands and drove through the gate of the château, anxious to prepare the lunches on time.

Over the last few days she'd been sifting through the library books, labeling the boxes to be put in their proper sections at a later date. There'd been many interesting finds, but so far she hadn't found anything to do with the Fleury family history. Perhaps by the time she left France, she'd come across something valuable to Alex personally.

As for the gorgeous owner of the estate, she'd seen him coming and going, but he'd been more preoccupied than usual and was out in the orchard at all hours. Sensing his urgency to be finished with the outside work, she'd come up with a plan to help him whether he liked it or not.

CHAPTER EIGHT

DANA went upstairs to change into jeans and a T-shirt. After removing the bracelet and putting it away, she slipped on her sneakers and hurried back to the kitchen. As soon as the baskets were ready, Dana took her father's to the grand salon and left it for him, then she went outside the front door with Alex's basket.

While she'd been in town, she'd turned in her rental car on a rental truck. It was only a half-ton pickup, not as big as Alex's, but it could hold a lot. She'd bought some gloves and was ready to roll. After climbing inside the cab, she drove around the back of the château to deliver his lunch.

She saw him loading a huge pile of branches and debris into his truck, more than it could possibly hold. Pleased to have arrived at an opportune moment, she pulled up on the other side of the pile.

Too bad she didn't have her camera so she could capture the stunned look on his burnished face. He paused in his work. "Do I dare ask what this is all about?"

Pleased that he didn't seem angry she said, "I traded in the rental car on this rental. It's my birthday and I want to do something that will make me happy. If you'll just let me help you haul this stuff away, it'll make my day. I'm a California girl and we love the sun."

"I haven't had an offer like that in a long time."

"Good." She slipped on the gloves and climbed out of the cab with his basket. "I'll put this in your truck. You can eat it on the way to the landfill." Dana felt his piercing gaze travel over her body. If he was wondering how long she'd last, she would prove she wasn't afraid of hard work.

Some of the branches were too heavy for her, but for the most part she was able to fill up the back of her truck with hefty tosses. When she saw how fast the pile was disappearing, she wished she'd thought of doing this a week ago.

"You keep up that pace and you'll wear yourself out."

"I'll take a rest when I need to," she assured him. They both continued working until the pile had disappeared. "Let's go dump all this stuff.

I'll follow you." She climbed in the cab and started the engine.

The last thing she saw was his dazzling white smile before he got in his truck and took off around the château. This was so much fun, she didn't want it to end. Being with Alex made her happy. It didn't matter what they were doing.

By the end of the day they'd made six more hauls, turning out double the work in half the time. When they returned and she parked the truck in front, he drew up next to her. In two seconds he walked over and pulled her out of the seat into his arms.

"You're hired," he murmured against her neck. His slight growth of beard tickled.

She tightened her arms around his broad chest. "I hope you mean that because I intend to help you until I leave."

His lips roved over her sunburned features before plundering hers. They drank from each other's mouths over and over. Their bodies clung. She relished his warmth that combined with his own male scent. Both were hot, thirsty and tired. Dana had never looked worse, but the way he was kissing her made her feel beautiful. She'd never felt beautiful before.

"You deserve a long soak in the tub, but make

it a short one. Meet me in the foyer in a half hour. I've been looking forward to our Scrabble game and don't want you falling asleep on me after dinner."

"I can't give you beautiful in half an hour, but I'll be clean."

"Then you don't mind if I don't shave?"

She smiled up into his eyes. "I like it. With that five o'clock shadow, no one would ever mistake you for our dull boy Jack." She kissed the corner of his jaw one more time before tearing herself out of his arms.

Thirty minutes later she hurried down the staircase in sandals, wearing a khaki skirt toned with a summery tan-and-white striped blouse that tied at the side of the waist. Her hair was still damp from washing it. She'd brushed it into some semblance of order. With an application of tangerine lipstick, she was ready.

Dana's heart was pounding far too fast. She would never be this age again and she would never have a birthday like this again with a man who could thrill her inside and out the way Alex did.

As he stepped out of his office and beckoned her inside, her legs turned to mush because he was so dark and handsome. He'd put on a cream polo shirt and tan trousers. "We match," she quipped to cover her emotions at being invited in the room where he worked and slept.

"I thought we'd eat in here tonight."

The interior came as total surprise because he'd surrounded himself with modern furniture. Amazingly it was like the kind in her parents' home in Hollywood. She glanced at him. "I take it you had all this shipped here?"

He nodded. "From Bali. Pieces of mine and my parents'. When I come in this room, it helps remind me I'm not a seventeenth-century man."

"I see what you mean. The château's atmosphere can swallow you alive. Every time I go to bed upstairs, I feel caught between two worlds."

She wandered over to an end table next to the leather couch where a framed picture was displayed. Dana studied it for a minute. "You get your height and bone structure from your father, but your coloring is all Fleury like your mother. They're very attractive people, Alex."

"Thank you. I think so, too. Will the birthday girl join me?" He held out a chair for her at a round game table made of mahogany. On the top he'd set up the Scrabble board. Next to the table was a tea cart with plates of club sandwiches, fruit and sodas. She noticed there was a supply of chocolate cookies for dessert.

Once she was seated she said, "I'm so glad we're not having oxtail or pickled pigs feet tonight."

He sat across from her, leveling a devilish glance at her. "After the hours of work you put in today, I wouldn't have done that to you. Help yourself to the food and we'll get started on our game."

Alex had made this casual and easy. She loved him for it. "I'll confess I haven't played this in years."

He sent her a sly smile.

For the next two hours they laughed and ate and played and fought over words they both made up when all else failed. Alex won every round.

"You're too good."

"I had to be in order to keep up with my father."

"Do you know my dad and I never played a board game of any kind? He simply didn't have the patience." Since her mother died, he hadn't had the time.

Alex eyed her steadily. "Some minds are too lofty."

"I think he was just scared to lose," she lied.

He chuckled. "It takes all types."

She nodded, wishing she could fall asleep in his arms.

"You look ready to nod off. Before you do, I have a present for you." He reached under the tea cart and handed her a wrapped gift. She assumed it was a book.

"This is exciting. Thank you."

Though Alex lounged back in the rattan chair, she sensed an intensity emanating from him while he waited for her to undo it. At first she didn't know what to think. The book was about an inch thick and bound in a dull red cloth. No title. It reminded her of an old chemistry lab notebook.

Curious, she opened the cover. Inside the paper had a slight yellow tinge. The French writing and notations, many of them numerical, had been penned in bold black ink. If anything it looked like an account ledger of some kind. She lifted her head to stare at Alex. "What is this?"

"You were so anxious to find something from the wine cellar, I rummaged through a couple of boxes upstairs you haven't opened yet and came across this book kept by one of the Belles Fleurs vintners."

"Alex—" she cried with excitement. "So not everything was thrown out."

"Evidently not. If you'll look down the left

side, you'll see the notations for 1902. I'm sure there are other books."

"I wish I could read French well enough to decipher this."

"Let me translate a little for you." He got up from the table and came around to stand behind her. With one arm encircling her left shoulder, he used his right index finger to show her each line as he explained in English. His chin was buried in her hair, sending little bursts of delight through her body.

"June—at the critical moment when the buds burst forth, the rain throughout the month produced irregular flowering. Bunches of grapes emerged stillborn.

"July—mildew has been a problem. The rain has continued causing the Layon to flood its banks. We removed the excess leaves from the west side of the plants to allow any sun to shine on the maturing fruit. We eliminated some bunches that flowered improperly in hope that the remaining clusters would ripen completely.

"'August—the hard labor is nearly done. The weather has turned hot and sunny. We have hopes some of the vintage will be saved. God grant us a few more dry weeks. By September we could have fruit. June makes the quantity. August makes the quality. We will see.'"

She shook her head. "I can't believe it. To think he's talking about the vineyard out there. *Your* vineyard! This is like a voice reaching out from the past. It gives me chills."

"Me, too," he murmured deep in his throat. It sent delicious vibrations through her nervous system. "Let's get more comfortable and we'll read a few more pages."

They gravitated to the comfy couch. He pulled her down on his lap, cocooning her so her head lay against his shoulder. Page by page he read to her, giving them insight into the struggles and joys of a vintner's work. The whole process was incredibly complicated. Much more so than she would ever have imagined.

His low masculine voice was so pleasant on her ear, she never wanted him to stop. Her eyelids started to feel heavy. She tried to stay awake, afraid to miss anything he told her.

"You're falling asleep."

"No, I'm not. Please don't make me move."

He pressed his mouth to hers. "I won't."

She yearned toward him. "I love it when you kiss me."

"I love to kiss you. The shape of your mouth is like the heart of a rose. It was made for me."

"Don't leave me." Her need for him had turned into an unbearable ache.

"I don't intend to."

Dana melted into him, trying to absorb his very essence until she knew no more.

The next time she became aware of her surroundings it was morning. She discovered herself on top of her bed in the same clothes she'd had on last night minus her sandals, covered by the duvet. She remembered nothing after she'd curled up against Alex.

It meant he'd carried her all the way up the stairs and down the hall to her room. And *that* after he'd put in ten hours of hard labor and prepared her birthday dinner.

As she sat up, she saw her present on the table next to the bed. Alex intended her to keep it, otherwise he wouldn't have brought it upstairs with her. She was touched beyond words, but at the same time it meant the book didn't have the significance for him it had for her. He had no qualms about her taking it with her when the company left for Germany.

A psychiatrist probably had a term for her

wanting Alex to care about his own property when it had nothing to do with her.

She rolled out of bed and changed into another pair of jeans and a jade top. As she put on her sneakers, a few new aches in her arms and back reminded she'd put in some hard physical work yesterday. There would be more today. She couldn't wait. It meant being with Alex.

After she'd freshened up in the bathroom, she went downstairs to get some breakfast. He was already in the kitchen. She felt his gaze staring at her over the rim of his orange juice glass. "Sleeping Beauty awake at last."

"I'm sorry I passed out on you last night. That last long walk carrying me must have been a backbreaker."

His dark eyes were smiling. "Not even love's first kiss could waken you, but I'm not complaining."

For an odd reason she felt shy around him all of a sudden. "Thank you for a wonderful birthday. I'll never forget it." She reached for an apple and bit into it.

"I won't, either. I've never seen a woman work as hard as you do."

"Mother said it's the Swede in me."

She would never know what he was going to

say next because Paul came in the kitchen looking for Alex.

"I'm glad I caught you before you went outside to work. For the next two days we'll be shooting some scenes here in the kitchen. They'll be night takes. The set director will want to come in here around 7:00 p.m. each evening to get everything organized. Will that be a problem for you?"

Alex shook his head. "Not at all. It will give me an excuse to play." His probing gaze swerved to Dana. "Mademoiselle Lofgren has accused me of being a dull boy. Two nights should give me enough time to rectify her poor opinion."

Paul winked at her. "Just don't let your dad know."

"What shouldn't I know?"

Dana jerked around in time to see her father enter the kitchen looking like thunder. Paul was quick on the uptake. "It's a joke between your daughter and me. Lighten up, Jan. It's only eight-thirty and we've got a whole day and night to get through." He disappeared out the door.

Her father walked over to her. "I need to talk to you in private, Dana. This is crucial." He flicked Alex a glance. "If you'll excuse us."

"Of course."

Disappointment swamped Dana. She'd planned to help Alex outside until time to fix the lunches. The absolute last thing she wanted to do was damage control for her father. He must have rattled one of the actors. Unfortunately when her father lost his temper, the ground shook and he used Dana to placate injured feelings.

Her gaze darted briefly to Alex before she left the kitchen.

When she found out what her father wanted, she hurried to find Paul. "Do me a favor?"

"Anything if it will put your father in a better mood. He and David don't usually quarrel."

"It's Dad. When he decides he wants something at the last minute, there's no dealing with him on a rational basis. I'm going to be gone for the next few days. Until I'm back, will you arrange for lunches to be brought in for him and Alex? Ask someone to take his out back and put it on his truck where he'll see it?"

"Sure."

"Thanks, Paul. Just hope I come back with good news."

"Amen."

Three more trees and the orchard would be cleared out. Alex drove his truck around the back of the château and got started on the first one. While he worked, he listened for Dana's truck. When she'd come in the kitchen this morning, she'd been dressed for work and his anticipation was growing.

After yesterday's experience he was spoiled and wanted her around every minute of the day and night, but several hours went by with no sign of her. Being employed by her father, naturally he had first call on her time. Where she was concerned, Alex had no rights at all.

Over the last few weeks he'd been listening between the lines. To his chagrin it appeared she'd be ready to move on to Germany at the end of the month, which was coming up too fast.

Lines bracketed his mouth. Regardless of her wanting to be independent, he noticed how quickly she jumped when her father snapped his fingers. Keeping in mind what Paul had told him, it made sense she continued to work with her father in order to study his directing skills.

Suddenly his saw slipped because he wasn't paying attention. He let go with a curse when he realized a couple of teeth had nicked him on the left forearm. Nothing major, but he needed a cloth to staunch the bleeding.

"Hello, Alex."

He stepped off the ladder to see Saskia Brusse, of all people, waiting for him with a large sack in her hand. "*Bonjour*, Mademoiselle Brusse."

"I'd say this was perfect timing. Did you know you're bleeding?"

"That's why I came down from the tree."

"I think there are some napkins in here that will stop it." She opened the sack and produced several.

"Thank you. Just what I needed." He pressed the paper napkins against it. Just as he thought, the cuts were mere surface wounds.

"You're welcome. Paul asked me to bring you lunch from the Hermitage. Mind if I stay out here and talk to you while you eat?" The brunette flashed him a smile that said she knew she was a knockout. Alex agreed, but he had other plans. He intended to find out why Dana hadn't come.

"I'm sorry, but I'm headed to the landfill." He climbed in the truck and closed the door. "It's been a pleasure talking to you, *mademoiselle*. I thank you and Paul for remembering me. Now, if you'll excuse me, I need to get back to work."

"But you've hardly taken any time off—"

"I can't afford to. There's still the under-growth around the sides and the front of the château to get rid of."

For the rest of the day he worked steadily until the last tree had been pruned. When he returned from his last haul, it was six-thirty. Dana had to be doing an errand for her father because her truck wasn't out in front.

Paul was just heading out with some others in the minivan. Alex slowed down so they could talk. "I appreciated the lunch."

"No problem. Dana will be back in a few days."

Back? He struggled to control his shock. "Where did she go?"

"Maille."

Alex had to reach back in his mind. "As in the Maille massacre?"

The other man nodded. "It's near Tours. At the last minute Jan decided he wants to film a small segment there. She's gone ahead to make the arrangements."

"Understood." Swallowing his bitter disap-pointment, he drove on around the back of the château.

Dana could have told him. She could have asked him to drive her there, but she wouldn't do that. It wasn't in her nature. If he asked her about it, she'd say that she knew he needed to finish his work.

Before he got out of the truck, he phoned her. With the orchard finished, he'd take the time off. He needed her… But with each attempt to reach her, he got the message "no service." She'd turned off her phone!

In his gut he got the disturbing sensation she was intentionally separating herself from him. Was this her way of letting him down? Cut him off at the ankles and chop away slowly until there was nothing left by the time the company moved on to Germany? Was it of her own free will because she had a career to pursue and didn't need a complication like Alex?

Another colorful expletive escaped his lips.

He could go after her and search until he found her, but that would mean asking Paul to be in charge of the estate until Alex returned. He couldn't do that. The man was under enough stress with Jan in one of his dark moods, but no mood could be as black as Alex's right now….

Thursday morning Dana got up early and left her hotel in Maille for Rablay. It had felt like months instead of three days since she'd seen Alex. By ten o'clock she could hardly breathe as she pulled around the side of the château and saw him making inroads on the vegetation between it and the winepress building. That meant he'd finished the orchard!

Panic set in. Whether he made enough money to pay the back taxes or not, she feared his days in France were numbered.

Trembling with excitement to see him again, she climbed out of the cab and hurried over to the area where he was working on the ladder. She stood at the base and looked up, feasting her eyes on his well-honed physique.

"Pardon, monsieur," she said in her best French, which she knew was terrible. "I'm looking for a man named Prince Charming. Could you tell me where he is?"

His hands stilled on the branch he was cutting before he looked down and slanted her a dark, piercing glance. "I'm afraid he only lives in a fairy tale."

She swallowed hard because that remote veneer he sometimes retreated behind was in evidence. "Spoilsport," she teased, hoping to inject a little levity into the conversation. "You're so grumpy I think you've been missing my lunches."

"Saskia has done her best to make up for them."

Not Mademoiselle Brusse any longer? Somehow Dana hadn't expected that salvo. "She loves to fuss for people who appreciate it. If you'll be nice to me, I have a little present for you. It only cost me ten Eurodollars."

"Is it something to eat?" She thought he might be thawing.

"No."

"To read?"

She smiled. "No."

"I give up. Why don't you bring it to me?"

Flame licked through her. "Am I talking to the same man who terrified me last time I tried it? For self-preservation I think you'll have to wait until you come down later. After I run inside for a few minutes, I'll be back out to help you."

She made it as far as the kitchen when she felt his hands on her arms. He spun her around. Their bodies locked, causing her to gasp. His expression looked borderline primitive. "Why did you turn off your phone?"

They were both out of breath. "So my father couldn't bark at me the whole time I was in Maille. I know when I shouldn't invade his space, but when I'm doing business for him, he doesn't recognize boundaries where I'm concerned."

There was a bluish-white ring around his lips.

"You didn't say goodbye." He gave her a gentle shake. "Not one phone call to let me know you were all right."

His words came as a revelation. "I—I wanted to call you, but I hated to bother you."

"Bother me?" he blurted. "By *not* phoning you've caused me two sleepless nights!"

"I'm sorry. I—"

But nothing else came out because his mouth had descended, devouring her with a hunger she'd only dreamed about. He crushed her against him, filling her with a voluptuous warmth. She swayed, almost dizzy from too much passion.

"While you were gone I almost went out of my mind," he whispered against her mouth before plundering it again. His lips caressed her eyes, her nose, her throat. He left a trail of fire everywhere there was contact.

"Don't you know I missed you, too?" She'd been living to be in his arms again.

"I don't even want to think about what it will be like when you're not around here anymore."

Dana heard the words, but their significance took a little time to sink in. If she understood him correctly, no matter how much he was attracted to her—no matter how much he wanted her and would miss her—when the time came, he was prepared to watch her disappear from his life.

His past relationships had never lasted, yet she wagered every woman who'd loved him still bore the scars of a broken heart. She'd known it would happen to her even before her father had warned her of the perils of staying at the château.

Calling on some inner strength, she cupped his arresting face in her hands. "Well, I'm back for now and I'm dying to give you your present."

Those dark eyes played over her features with relentless scrutiny. "Where is it?"

"In my purse."

"I don't see it."

"It dropped to the floor when you caught up to me."

He pressed another urgent kiss to her mouth before releasing her to pick it up.

"Can I look inside?"

"Go ahead."

His hand produced a sack. He held it up. "Is this it?"

She nodded. "I didn't have time to get it gift wrapped." Dana reached inside the sack and pulled out a hat. "Here—let me put it on you."

His brow quirked. "You bought me a beret?"

"Not any beret. This comes from Maille. I came across a shop that makes these in remembrance of the men of the Resistance in the early days of the war. The proceeds go to a memorial fund for the victims' families who were massacred."

She placed it on his head at a jaunty angle. "You're a handsome man, you know, and the beret adds a certain *je ne sais quoi*." She stared at him for a moment, trying to recover from her near heart attack. "Every Frenchman should look as good."

He paraded in front of her like a French soldier. "You think?" His disarming smile brought her close to a faint.

"You should listen to Dana. She knows what she's talking about."

They both turned to see the renowned French film star standing inside the entrance to the kitchen. Who knew how long she'd been observing them?

Dana smiled at her. "Simone? Please meet Alexandre Fleury Martin, the owner of the estate who made this location possible for us to rent. Alex? This is Simone Laval."

"Enchante, mademoiselle. I saw one of your French films when my family lived in La Cote D'Ivoire. You're an excellent actress, very

intense. My mother was a fan of yours. If she were alive today, she'd love to meet you."

As Dana digested that bit of information, the actress's warm, sherry-brown eyes played over him in genuine female interest. "Call me Simone, and the pleasure is all mine."

Simone was still in her 1940s clothes and makeup. Obviously Dana's father had given everyone a break to use the restrooms or go outside to smoke.

As she shook hands with Alex, their conversation switched to French. Dana could tell he was totally taken with the winning charm of the thirty-eight-year-old divorcée. What male wasn't attracted to her? With her dark auburn hair, she was a natural-born beauty. A real babe, as the guys on the crew referred to her.

The two of them looked good together. Some people meshed on a first meeting. Dana could tell there was a spark between them. Maybe it was their Gallic connection. Whatever, she saw it in the attitudes of both their bodies. They were so intent on each other, Dana slipped unnoticed from the kitchen.

Her father expected a report on the trip. Now that she was back, she might as well do it while he was waiting to resume the filming.

CHAPTER NINE

"SHALL we go?" Alex cupped Dana's elbow and ushered her out of the movie theater to his truck. After a hard day's work hauling more debris, it had been heavenly to drive into town with him for dinner and a film.

"How did you like the *Da Vinci Code*?" Though it had been out for four years, he hadn't seen it. Now that they were headed home from Angers, she was curious to know his reaction.

He flashed her a curious glance. "I found the mixture of fact and fiction riveting, but I'm much more interested to hear what you thought about it."

"Why?"

His hand squeezed hers a little harder. "Come on, Dana. We both know the answer to that."

She heard an edge in his tone and was stunned by it. "We do? Perhaps you better tell me because I've forgotten."

"A while back Paul confided that you have plans to be a director. Today Simone confirmed it."

Dana was surprised Paul had said anything. She was even more surprised the subject had come up in Alex's conversation with Simone. Disturbed in a strange way, she removed her hand from his warm grasp. "What exactly did she tell you?"

"So you don't deny it."

A heavy sigh escaped her lips. "Alex—what's this all about?" How could such a perfect night have turned into something that created so much tension in him?

"Simone said that your input during several of the scenes at the film studio were so insightful, your father didn't contradict you. I've been thinking about that. If he didn't trust your directing instincts, he wouldn't send you off to arrange film locations for him."

"Before Mother died, she and I did it together."

"But you're the one with the talent."

She lowered her head. "Why do I get the feeling you're accusing me of something?" Out of the corner of her eye she saw his hands tighten on the steering wheel.

"Because when we first met, you misrepresented yourself."

The heat of anger prickled. "In what way?"

"You intimated you were at your father's beck and call, nothing more. In reality you're being groomed by him because he accepts directing as your destiny."

What? "Surely you're joking—" she cried in astonishment.

"Not at all. At first I saw his possessiveness as a desperate attempt not to lose you after your mother passed away." She couldn't believe what she was hearing. "However, in light of what I've learned, I've had to rethink that supposition."

"And what conclusion have you arrived at exactly?" came her brittle question.

"He's hated my guts from day one because he doesn't want anything to get in the way of a brilliant career for you. Your father sees me as a possible threat."

Her pain was escalating in quantum leaps. "But since you and I know that's not the case, there's no point to this conversation. I don't understand what you have against the art of film directing. To each his own, I guess."

He muttered something dampening in French.

"As long as it's question time, why didn't

you ask Simone to dinner tonight instead of me? Before Paul left the château earlier this evening, he indicated she's more than a little interested in you. I would have thought you'd love to spend time with such a lovely compatriot."

By now they'd arrived at the front of the château. He slammed on the brakes and turned to her. In the semi-darkness his features took on an almost menacing cast. "You'd like that, wouldn't you?"

She jerked her head toward him. "It's not my place to like or dislike what you do. When you said I could stay at the château, it was understood we were both free agents, able to come and go with no strings. You made that emphatically clear when you refused to accept the bottle of wine I bought you out of friendship."

His sharp intake of breath sounded louder in the confines of the cab.

"Why you're coming at me with this inquisition is beyond me. I've had enough. If you don't mind, I'm tired and need to go to bed."

"But I do mind—" He leaned across her to lock the door so she couldn't get out.

"I want the truth." His lips were mere centimeters from hers, but instead of kissing them, he was being relentless with his questions. "Are you planning to direct films in the future?"

Being a director might have appealed to her once, but after the Neal fiasco she realized she didn't want to be associated with the film world in any sense. Too many narcissists to deal with, too many artistic temperaments, too much blind ambition. But if she told Alex that, he would continue to believe what he wanted, so it wasn't worth the effort.

"I guess when Dad thinks I'm ready." Not only was it the answer he seemed determined to hear, but it would send the message that she had other things on her mind besides him after she left France. "May I get out now?"

Lines had darkened his face. He studied her through narrowed lids as if he'd been gauging the veracity of her words. "Not yet. A few weeks ago I asked you about the plot of this film. You held back on me. Simone told me the film was really your inspiration. She said you know every line and verse of it, that in fact, you helped write part of the script with David."

"What if I did?"

He sucked in his breath. "Why couldn't you have shared that with me?"

If she told him the truth now, that she'd been

trying to be a mystery woman to arouse his interest, he would know she was desperately in love with him.

Deep down he already knew it, but she wasn't about to give him the satisfaction of hearing the words. Not when he was prepared to see her drive away from the château next Monday, never to return.

"Most people don't really want to hear the answer to the questions they ask," she theorized.

He sat back with a grimace. "You put me in that category?"

"I didn't know you that well."

She saw his jaw harden. "You do now. I'd like to hear the story."

"Wouldn't you rather see the film when it comes out and be surprised?"

"No," he muttered. "I don't like surprises."

Dana averted her eyes. "I know."

"I wasn't referring to your gifts. I like my hat," he added in a gentler tone.

So did she. On *him*. "Let's go inside first." Their bodies were too close here in the cab.

Once he'd helped her down, she walked to the front door ahead of him. After he opened it and turned on lights, she made a beeline for the kitchen and took a soda out of the fridge. Small as it was, it provided the symbolic armor she needed to keep him at a distance. Or rather, keep her from him.

He made instant coffee, then lounged against the counter to sip it while he stared at her. "I'm waiting."

"Why are you so interested?"

"How could I not be when you picked my estate out of all the French possibilities?"

She supposed he had a point there. "The story calls for a setting where a German soldier, that would be Rolfe Meuller, refuses to be a part of the Maille massacre of August in 1944 in the Loire Valley. It happened on the day Paris was liberated from German occupation.

"His superior shoots him and he's left for dead. Later on he's discovered barely alive, having dragged himself to the garden of a nearby château that has suffered through two world wars and has been raided for its wine. Perhaps now that I've given you a few details, you understand why I knew the moment I glimpsed the château for the first time that it was perfect. Uncannily so."

Alex nodded.

"A young, aristocratic French woman, the

second wife of her military husband who's been stationed in Paris for months, comes across his body. That would be Simone.

"He's very attractive. She's never been able to have children and has been trapped in a loveless marriage. The handsome blond German is someone's son and that sentiment causes her to help him.

"As you might assume, when he starts to heal from his wounds, she wants him to become her lover. That places him in a difficult position because he has a wife he loves, yet this French woman could turn him over to the Vichy French or the Germans at any time. He must find a way to placate her until he can walk on his own and escape.

"To stall for time, he uses psychology to get her to talk to him. The film explores both their psyches, exposing their tortured souls. His agony over the senseless murders and killings in the French town is the focus of the story.

"When she agrees to let him go and not tell the authorities, he makes it back to his wife in Germany. That would be Saskia. Their reunion is tragic because she's had a baby and it isn't his. She's burdened by her own guilt. He's broken by man's inhumanity to man at Maille, torn up over her infidelity and mourning his wasted life in a hideous war.

"They can continue on together, bound by their individual Gethsemanes, or they can go their separate ways. The film forces you to decide what they might or might not do. The viewer will have to examine his or her own soul for the most palatable answer."

He drank the rest of his coffee. "It's going to be a powerful film. Where did the kernel of the idea come from?" Alex used her former words to frame his question.

She tossed her empty can in the wastebasket. "There was a picture of Sarkozy in the newspaper. He was in Maille to honor the victims. I showed it to Dad and we discussed the massacre. Before I knew it, he'd dreamed up a basic storyline. That's how it came into being."

"With all your contributions, will your name be listed in the credits?"

"No. Make no mistake. This is Dad's picture. He's getting a masterful performance out of Rolfe Mueller, an unknown. When the film's released, he'll be a star."

She moved to the doorway. "As for you, your estate will be immortalized. By the time you have it ready for the public to visit, the stream of tourists will be never ending and make you a rich man. Good night, Alex. Thank you for dinner and the movie."

He didn't try to detain her. His nonaction sent another jab of pain to her shattered heart.

Dana didn't sleep well. In the early morning, she went up to the third floor with the intention of opening more boxes and labeling them. However, there was still so many to do and Alex appeared so uninterested in her project, she decided there was no point in going on.

She put the chair she'd borrowed back in the other room and took all her tools back to the bedroom. Restless and dissatisfied, she showered and dressed in fresh jeans and a T-shirt.

For the next two hours she would help Alex haul debris before she had to make the lunches. But in that regard she was stymied because his truck wasn't there and he hadn't left any piles for her to work on. She was so used to knowing where he was at all times, it upset her to find him gone.

At noon she packed the baskets, but he still hadn't returned. She left her father's in its usual spot and Alex's in the kitchen. When one o'clock rolled around and he still hadn't appeared, she went back upstairs to scour the bathroom and leave it as spotless as she'd found it weeks ago.

Her bedding and the bathroom towels belonged to Alex. He wouldn't mind if she used his appliances to get them washed and dried. By three she'd housecleaned the bedroom and had packed up everything.

Dana hadn't intended to move out of the château until tomorrow morning, but it was better this way. No goodbye scene.

On her way out of the side entrance to the truck, she thought about the bottle of Belles Fleurs wine resting down in the wine cellar. Much as she wanted to take it home as a souvenir, she knew it belonged here. Alex had given her the vintner notebook. That would have to be enough.

One more day's filming on Monday and everyone would clear out. Alex would get his château back. Dana's part was done. Her father wouldn't be able to fault her for anything, that is if she even figured in the recesses of his mind.

She put her suitcase on the floor of the cab and took off. If by any chance she and Alex crossed paths, she would tell him she had an errand to do for her father. He wouldn't question it. If he wanted to make plans for the evening, she'd tell him she'd get back to him when she knew something more definite.

Part of her was praying she'd see him coming so she could feast her eyes on him one last time, but it didn't happen. She found herself en route to Paris, free as a bird and filled with the most incredible loneliness she'd ever known.

There was a flight leaving Orly airport tonight for St. Louis. From there she'd take another flight to Los Angeles. The trick was to return the truck to the car rental in time to get through the check-in line.

While she maneuvered in and out of heavy traffic, she phoned her father. He'd be through filming for the day. His phone rang several times. Finally, "Dana?"

"Hi, Dad."

"I'm glad it's you. I just received another call from Monsieur Dumarre. He wants to be sure you're coming to the vintner party tomorrow night he's giving for Alex. After the filming is over tomorrow, we'll drive back to the hotel while I get dressed, then we'll go to his home from there."

The vintner party…Alex hadn't brought it up in days. Another hurt.

"Dad—I'm afraid you'll have to take Saskia with you."

"It's over with her. I want to take my daughter."

He wanted her mother. Dana was the next best thing. Her eyes smarted. "You don't understand. I'm on my way back to California as we speak."

A long silence ensued. "What's going on?"

"I told you the other day. I've got to make my own life. It's time. But I'm hoping you'll do me one favor."

He didn't respond because for once she'd shocked him, but she knew he was listening.

"Please go to the party and take Saskia. Do it to support Alex. H-he's a good man. The best there is." Her voice trembled. "Be nice to him."

"Dana—"

She hung up. For the first time in her life she'd cut him off. It was the beginning of many firsts to find her life. One that would never include Alex Fleury Martin.

If you could die from loving someone too much, she was a prime candidate.

After being in meetings all day, Alex arrived back at the château at seven-thirty, anxious to talk to Dana. No vehicles were parked out front. He drove around the side, hoping to see her truck. It wasn't there.

He let himself in the side door. Only when he saw the basket with his lunch still sitting on the counter did he realize he should have called her and told her he'd gotten hung up on business.

She'd packed some plums. He sank his teeth into one while he waited for her to answer her phone. The caller ID indicated no service. Not to be daunted, he strode through the château to his office and looked up Paul's phone number. He'd know where to find her.

Unfortunately all he got was his voice mail. Alex imagined everyone was out having dinner since it was a Friday night. He left Paul the message to phone him ASAP.

There was a voice mail for Alex from Monsieur Dumarre. The other man had called to remind him of tomorrow's party. He mentioned that Jan Lofgren was coming and would be bringing Dana.

Alex had his own ideas on that score. That was why he needed to talk to Dana. He was taking her to the party and had plans for them afterward. If she insisted she couldn't leave her father, then the three of them would go together and the hostile director would have to handle it!

After making the rounds of the château to lock doors and turn out lights, he returned to the kitchen. He'd had a big meal in Angers with his friend from Louisiana who'd flown in at Alex's request, but he was still craving something sweet, like her mouth. Where was she? Why hadn't she called him?

He poked around in the basket and found a *petit pain au chocolat*. A smile broke out on his face. She had as bad a sweet tooth as he did. In two bites he devoured the whole thing.

Finally desperate, he phoned the Hermitage and asked to be connected to Monsieur Lofgren's room. Again he was shut down when there was no answer and he was told to leave a message. Alex chose not to. If he didn't hear from Dana in another hour, he'd phone her father again.

Maybe the whole company was out celebrating tonight, including Dana. This would be their last weekend in the Anjou before they left for either Maille or the Rhine.

Another film company from Lyon would be arriving in a week for a four-day shoot, followed by the Paris outfit scheduled for mid-September and another for the first two weeks of October.

Every few days he was getting more feelers from his ad. Business was starting to pick up. After talking with his banker today, the outlook was promising that he'd be able to pay the first increment of back taxes by the November deadline.

When he'd come up with this insane scheme, he hadn't really believed it would work, but he'd been out of any other ideas. Then Dana had come trespassing on his property like a mischievous, adorable angel. Her presence had turned his whole life around until he didn't know himself anymore.

The next two hours passed like two years. He was driven to watch TV. No one phoned. He called the Metropole and asked them to ring Dana's room. No answer. Her father wasn't back in his room.

Feeling borderline ferocious over the way his evening had turned out, he took a cold shower before going back to his room. Dana was an early bird. He planned to be up and waiting for her when she drove in from town with the others.

As he entered the bedroom his cell phone rang. It was Paul.

"Thanks for calling me back."

"It sounded important. I'm sorry I didn't check my phone sooner."

"No problem. I was looking for Dana."

"To my best knowledge she's in Paris, seeing about one of the locations there in case Jan decides to add a small scene. He always keeps his options open and nobody negotiates like Dana. She ought to be back some time tomorrow."

All this time she'd been in Paris and unavailable….

"Thanks for the information. Good night, Paul."

The last thing he noticed before turning off the lamp was the beret he'd put on the dresser. Alex comforted himself with the fact that a woman didn't buy a man something like that unless she meant it.

When he awakened the next morning, his first thought was to check his phone in case Dana had called, but there were no messages. Eager to find out if she was back, he got dressed and rushed outside. Still no sign of her truck, either, in front or around the side.

By noon he'd lost all interest in work and decided to quit for the day. On his way down the ladder he heard his name called.

"Paul?"

"Hi. I brought you lunch."

"Where's Dana?" he fired before he realized he'd been rude.

"In Paris. She told Jan she'd meet you at the vintner party tonight. He asked me to pass that along."

Alex took the sack from him. He had to tamp down the surge of negative emotions tearing him apart. "Thanks for the information and the food."

"You're welcome."

Eight hours later Alex found himself in deep conversation with an enthusiastic crowd of the Anjou's most renowned vintners. Their genuine interest in Alex and their questions concerning his future plans for the estate were heartwarming to say the least.

But by halfway through the evening, Dana still hadn't arrived. Even Monsieur Dumarre, their congenial host who'd brought this very elite fraternity together seemed disappointed. Not even the presence of the famous Jan Lofgren made a difference. However, Dumarre's reaction couldn't match the black state Alex was in.

Dana would never have missed this without a compelling reason. She'd be in her element discussing the Fleury's former contribution to the wine world. Something was wrong. He'd sensed it in his gut since yesterday, but fool that he was, he'd been biding his time because he knew they'd have the rest of the night to themselves.

Being as polite as he could, he excused

himself from the crowd and made his way across the room to Jan, who was holding court to a cluster of fascinated listeners. Saskia was circulating with her own following. Without hesitation Alex walked up to him. "Jan? I have to talk to you now. Alone," he underlined.

The older man's frigid blue eyes met his head-on. He nodded and excused himself to everyone. They walked through some French doors to a veranda overlooking the back garden. For the moment no one else was out there.

Alex's hands formed fists. This confrontation had been coming on for a long time. "Where's Dana? I want the truth. So far both Paul and Mademoiselle Brusse have been lying for you so don't deny it."

Jan eyed him pensively. "In California."

Hearing it was like being dealt a body blow, rocking him on his heels. "On another errand for *you*?" His accusatory question hung in the air, sending out its own shock wave.

"No," came the quiet response. "She quit her job yesterday and plans to look for a new one."

"You mean, as an independent film director." No more tiptoeing around the almighty film director. It was past time to lay out the bare bones and be done with it.

To his astonishment, a strange light filled her father's eyes. Alex didn't know they could look like that. "She's good, but that doesn't appear to be her destiny after all."

The words shook him to the core. "What do you mean?"

"I mean, she's got too much of her mother in her—in my opinion the best part of her parents. I hope that answers your question because Saskia's signaling me to rejoin the others."

While Alex stood there in a shocked daze, Jan extended his hand, forcing him to shake it. "If I don't see you again before the company pulls out on Tuesday, I'd like to thank you. Not only for the loan of your magnificent château, but the generosity that went with it."

He cocked his balding head. "My daughter knew a good thing when she saw it."

As he walked away, Alex felt the world tilt. He'd fallen into quicksand of his own making.

When he drove hell-bent through the gate of the château an hour later and saw her truck parked in front, he feared he was hallucinating.

Dana heard Alex's truck before she saw it emerge from the trees. She knew it was impossible, but from the scream of the engine he sounded as if he was going a hundred miles an hour. When he applied the brakes, the truck skidded in a half circle before coming to a stop.

Out of the dust that went flying, he emerged from the cab, looking sinfully handsome in a formal dark blue suit. She'd never seen in him a dress shirt and tie before. He'd gotten a haircut. Not a lot had been removed, but enough to add to his sophistication.

Her mouth went dry because she loved him so much, but he looked terrifyingly angry. In seconds he'd stalked around her side of the truck and flung the door open. He braced his other hand against the frame so she couldn't get out. "I thought you were in California." His voice sounded as if it had come from a subterranean cavern.

Only one person knew her plans. That meant Alex and her father had crossed paths at the party. It would have been a fiery exchange. She shivered, moistening her lips nervously. "I changed my mind, but I got back from Paris too late to come to the party. H-how was it?" she stammered.

His dark eyes studied her with a veiled scrutiny that made the hairs stand on the back of her neck. "Most everyone seemed to have a good time with several exceptions, one of them being Monsieur Dumarre. You made a conquest of him. He was visibly disappointed when you didn't show up."

Dana's hand tightened on the steering wheel. "I'll make it up to him. What I want to know is if *you* had a good time."

"That's a hell of a question to ask since you provided the impetus for him to give the party at all!" he bit out. "Did I have a good time?" His question rent the air. "If you mean did I enjoy getting to meet the prominent vintners in the region and hear stories about the glory days of Belles Fleurs? Then yes, that part was satisfying."

She bit her lip. "Did you take Simone with you? She would have loved it."

Alex made a scathing sound in his throat. "The only star there was Saskia. I had no idea she was such an excellent actress. She managed to convey that you were off doing vital studio business no one else could do. Her performance to cover for your absence did her great credit."

Dana's father had no doubt choreographed Saskia's contribution. He'd actually pulled through for Dana. That was something to be thankful for at least. Alex's rage was another matter altogether.

"Are you always going to be angry with me because of it?"

"I don't know," his voice grated. "You're the one who got me into the predicament in the first place."

His arresting face was so close, she only had to move her hands a few inches and she could be touching him. "I'm sorry," she whispered.

"No, you're not."

Her head flew back. "You're right. I'm not sorry that because he found out you were a Fleury, he wanted to celebrate your arrival in Rablay with his friends. It was a great honor for you. I wish I'd been there. It's very upsetting to me that I wasn't, but it couldn't be helped." She stirred in place. "I'll find a way to apologize to him, whatever it takes."

The little pulse she'd seen before hammered at the corner of his taut mouth. "Your father told me you quit on him."

With that news out in the open, there were no secrets left. The exchange between them couldn't have been anything but ugly. "True. I'm now jobless and looking for a new career."

"With all your contacts, the field should be wide-open for you in California. Why didn't you get on the plane?"

Dana's lungs constricted. Holding her heart in her hands, she said, "While I was standing in line waiting to check my suitcase, it came to me what I really wanted to do with my life."

"Just like that—" he rapped out, sounding exasperated.

"Yes."

"I guess I shouldn't be surprised," he muttered. "It took you all of ten seconds to decide you wanted to rent the château for your father."

"When something becomes clear, I've found it's better not to hesitate."

"You mean, like charging up a ladder with no regard for your safety?"

Her eyes flashed sparks. "You're never going to let me forget that, are you? I can't help it that I inherited that trait from my mother."

She saw something flicker in the dark recesses of his eyes. "You still haven't answered my question."

"I'm getting to that. After I made my decision not to board the plane, I left the airport terminal and rented the truck back. But by the time I reached Angers, it was midnight. I was so exhausted I stayed at the Metropole and slept in late."

"You've been there all day?" He sounded livid.

"Yes. I had phone calls to make."

"Except to me." His words came out like a hiss.

"I couldn't call you until I'd worked everything out."

He made another violent sound that caused her to quiver. "But it didn't all mesh until it was too late to attend the party. Is that what you're saying?"

She nodded, afraid to look at him. "Could we go inside first?"

"If you'd come to the party, you could have savored dozens of the region's finest wines."

"I could have, but the one I wanted to taste wouldn't have been available. Or was it?" she questioned.

His dark brows lifted. "No. I'm afraid our kindhearted host wasn't willing to give up a second bottle of Belles Fleurs. But who's to say what he would have done if you'd been there…"

On that note he scooped her out of the seat and set her on the ground. In the moonlight she looked so frumpy standing next to him in her jeans and T-shirt, she could have wept. No words passed between them as he pulled her suitcase from the floor of the cab and followed her into the château.

CHAPTER TEN

DANA'S heart skipped a beat when Alex opened the door to the petit salon and turned on the light. "Wait for me in here. I'll be back with your drink."

In this mood, she didn't dare argue with him. Forcing herself not to look at the bedroom end of the room, she moved one of the rattan chairs over to the desk where he'd set up his computer.

Before long he was back. He strolled toward her and set the cola on the desk next to her. Still not saying anything, he shrugged out of his elegant suit jacket. Next came the tie. He tossed them over a nearby chair before undoing the top buttons of his shirt.

The dusting of black hair against his bronzed throat stood out in contrast to the dazzling white of the material. His male beauty caused her to gasp inwardly.

"You wouldn't rather sit on the couch where you'd be more comfortable?"

She'd been there and done that the other night, but everything had changed since then. "This is fine right here for the business I have in mind."

He removed his cuff links and pushed the sleeves up to the elbows, revealing more of his bronzed arms. She saw the gash on his arm. "You cut yourself! When did that happen?"

"Yesterday."

"With the saw?"

"It's nothing. Let's not get off topic. Are you telling me you came back to the château to talk business?"

"Yes. I've had a lot of time to think and— Alex? Will you please sit down? I can't think while you're looming over me like that."

"Is that what I'm doing?"

"Yes."

To her relief he sat down in his swivel chair, extending his long legs so his shoes touched her sneakers. She tucked her feet under her chair. "Is this better?"

"Much."

With one arm on the desk, he gazed at her through shuttered eyes. "How long are you going to keep me in suspense?"

"Not any longer, but you have to promise you won't interrupt until I'm through."

He folded his strong arms. "I'm waiting."

"This is serious now."

"I can see that."

She sat forward. "Please don't patronize me."

"I apologize if that's what it sounded like."

"Sorry. I'm a little touchy about that sort of thing." Dana had thought she could do this, but now that the moment had come, she was in agony. "I have to give you a little background first."

"You mean, there are things about you I still don't know?"

"Exactly. For instance my mother did most of the gardening when I was young. I liked to help her and took pride in the flower beds I planted and weeded. If someone were to ask what was the happiest time of my life, I would have to say it was out gardening, watching things grow. Being in the sun. A lot of beautiful flowers grow in Southern California. It's like a garden of Eden."

So far she seemed to be holding Alex's interest. "But at the time, I didn't consider it important work. Sometimes when I took dad his lunch at the studio, he'd let me stay on the set to watch. What he did seemed very important and I thought, one day I'll grow up to do what he does.

"Over the years I've been studying his technique. One day Paul and I were talking and I expressed my hope to become a director. When I asked him what he thought about it, he was quiet for a while, then he said, 'You're a natural at it, Dana, but I would worry about you because it's not a happy profession.'

"I knew that. My father was living proof he experienced a lot of difficult moments, but directing gave him an outlet for his artistic talent and that seemed very important.

"Little by little, Dad gave me more responsibilities to learn the craft. We often came at an idea the same way. After mother died he trusted me to do more for him. Scouting for unique locations was one example. Editing a script, making changes was another.

"I thought it was what I was truly *meant* to do. Yet in the back of my mind, Paul's comment continued to nag at me. I've kept asking myself if directing was what I *wanted* to do.

"That question got answered for me last week when I started helping you in the orchard. It has taken me back to those times when I helped Mother in the yard. There's nothing like hands-on experience working in the out-of-doors.

"Lately I've been looking at the overrun vegetable and flower gardens at the other end of the château. So many ideas of how to replant them and make the grounds beautiful is all I think about. When Dad sent me to Maille, I didn't want to go."

She paused to rub her eyes. "After this long, boring speech, what I'm trying to say is that I'd like to be the first person in line for the estate manager job."

He muttered a French imprecation she didn't need translated.

"Believe me, when word gets out you're looking for one before you leave for Louisiana, there'll be lines out to the street hoping for the privilege. I can't think of any career I'd love more than to be put in charge of this place after you've gone."

"It's a lot of hard work, Dana."

"I like hard work. Besides, it's one of the most beautiful spots in France. I'm in love with it. You could trust me to do a better job than anyone else."

Alex stared at her as if he'd never seen her before.

Taking advantage of the silence, she said, "Until that time, I'd like to apprentice for it. I'll do any jobs that need doing. I'll help you clean every room and bring down the furniture. I'd love to put the books in the library and catalog everything.

"I'll plant and weed. I'll pick fruit when the time comes. I realize there are dozens of things I don't know how to do, but I can watch and learn from you."

That remote look she hated crept over his face.

"Please don't close your mind to this, Alex—I know what you're going to say. That you don't have the money to pay me right now, but I don't want pay. One day when it's finally open to the public, we can talk about a salary. Don't you see there's nothing I'd like more than working here?"

He got to his feet.

Though it was nothing tangible, she realized she'd crossed a line with him that probably spelled disaster for her. Dana had known it would be a huge risk, but she'd been willing to take it.

She jumped out of her chair. "Just promise me you'll think about it and give me your answer in the morning. If it's no, I'll understand and leave."

Afraid he might tell her no right now, she grabbed her suitcase placed by the door and hurried out of the room toward the staircase. For the third time in three weeks she lugged it up the steps.

When she reached her room, she turned on the flashlight so she could see to get ready for bed. But she was too worked up to change yet and went over the window. Moonlight had turned the view of the Layon into a river of silver.

For a long time she stood there remembering the night they'd cleaned this fabulous room together, the fun they'd had buying her bed. Her mind was filled with memories of the nights he'd come in here to light the candles, bringing the kind of enchantment you could never find in a storybook.

Hot tears trickled out the corners of her eyes. As she turned away to open her suitcase, Alex appeared in the entry, looking so handsome she almost fainted. He was still wearing the same clothes and carried several things in his arms. Her heart almost leaped out of her chest.

"Don't be startled. I've come to give you your answer now."

It was darker on that side of the room. She moved toward him, but she still couldn't see what he'd put on the table. Maybe it was new candles, but when he walked toward her, carrying two half-full glasses of wine, anything she'd been thinking about left her mind.

The way he was staring at her, she honestly

couldn't catch her breath. "As interviews for a job go, yours was extraordinary," he began. "I'm very impressed you would forego a salary in order to learn how to be my manager, therefore, you're hired."

"You mean it?" she cried, hardly daring to believe it.

A ghost of a smile hovered around his lips. "Let's drink to your success, shall we?"

Alex was being very mysterious. It sent chills of excitement through her body. With a trembling hand, she took one of the wineglasses from him. He touched her rim with his and took a drink. She sipped hers, but the second the liquid ran down her throat she realized they weren't drinking Percher, Chaume, or any wine she'd ever tasted before.

Her eyes widened. "What domaine is this?" She took another sip. "The texture is so velvety. How could anything be this incredible? Can you taste that smoky sweetness?"

He nodded. "At the party I was told 1892 was a great vintage year."

When the meaning of his words got through, Dana almost dropped the glass. She stared at him in disbelief. "You opened the bottle!"

"You said you were waiting for an important

occasion. I would think taking on a new career constitutes as one. Don't you agree?"

Dana was in shock and could only nod her head. She took another drink. "The wine is out of this world. There's a richness that tastes of the earth itself."

"A nuance from the minerals. That's what comes from a hundred years of aging," he murmured.

Emotion caused her eyes to moisten. "To think we're drinking from your grapes that have been growing on Belles Fleurs soil for hundreds of years." She drank a little more. "Don't you feel a tingling to realize this is a tangible connection to your ancestors?"

"I feel a great deal more than that." He finished his wine and put both their glasses on the table. "While we were downstairs I forgot to tell you I met with my colleague from Louisiana yesterday. He's been anxious to know when I'm going to join him."

How odd she could go cold so fast when the wine had warmed her body clear through. "Did you tell him it won't be long now?"

"No. I informed him he'd have to find another agricultural engineer because France is home to me, permanently. I'm getting married."

Maybe she was dreaming.

"My bride-to-be and I have a life to live and a vineyard to work. Both need love and tender nurturing on a full-time basis."

"Alex—"

Her cry reverberated throughout the tower.

"I'm in love with you, Dana Lofgren. I have been from the beginning, but I sensed a battle with your father and was forced to bide my time before I made my move."

She launched herself into his arms, sobbing for happiness. "Oh, darling, I love you so much, you can't possibly imagine."

He rocked her body back and forth, kissing her hair, her face. "I think you convinced me downstairs."

"I couldn't leave you. When I was standing in that line at the airport, I felt I'd come to the end of my life."

Alex buried his face in her hair. "Try hearing your father tell me you'd gone to California."

She hugged him harder. "I'm sorry. I asked him to be nice to you, but I should have known better."

"You don't understand." He pulled back so he could look at her. "In his way, he gave me his blessing."

"What do you mean?" Her heart had started to thud.

He kissed the tears off her cheeks. "I was ready for a showdown with him until he told me something that changed everything. He said you'd make a good director, but it wasn't your destiny because you were too much like your mother."

"Dad admitted it?"

He nodded.

Dana was delirious with joy.

"Once I heard that, I couldn't get home from the party fast enough to collect a few things and go after you. If I hadn't seen your truck out in front, poor Paul would have gotten a phone call telling him to take care of everything while I was gone."

Dana slid her hands up his chest to his shoulders, relishing the right to touch him like this. "And I sat there terrified you'd drive in with Simone."

"Simone who?" he demanded fiercely, shaking her. "From the night you trespassed on my property, I haven't been the same. Sapto will tell you."

"Who's Sapto?"

"The house boy in Bali who got attached to me. You'll like him. He's saving his money to go to college. I'm planning to fly him over to help us prune the vineyard. That should give his earnings a boost.

"In my last postcard to him, I told him he can stop asking about all the women in my life because I've found the one I want."

Dana pressed a kiss to his lips, too euphoric to talk.

"When I stopped at the post office this afternoon, I discovered another postcard from him. He said that from my description of you, you would give me many beautiful children."

Alex's eyes narrowed on her mouth. "I knew it over dinner that night at the Hermitage. You sat there in the candlelight and your femininity reached out to me like a living thing. It came to me in a flash you were the one I was going to love for the rest of my life, to make babies with."

"I—I knew it before you did." Her voice caught. "From the first moment I laid eyes on you coming out of the shadows. This is going to sound silly, but it wasn't to me. Like Sleeping Beauty in reverse, I felt that I'd come upon the castle of the Sleeping Prince. Everything in me yearned toward you."

His smile turned her heart over. "So now we know the true story of Rapunzel."

She laughed softly, remembering their crazy talk. "She had no shame and moved in on her prince, sleeping bag and all."

"He liked her style." In the next breath Alex kissed her mouth hungrily. "How about taking a walk out to the vineyard with me? We have serious plans to make and fast, because I don't intend to make love to you until you're my wife. I promised your father."

"When?" she half groaned. "I didn't hear you."

"It wasn't anything verbal, but the commitment was just as binding the second you announced your plan to find a spot in the château to sleep."

Dana hid her face in his chest. "You must have thought I was out of my mind."

He tangled his fingers in her hair. "To be honest I thought heaven had dropped a present at my door by mistake, but I wasn't about to give it back and had to think fast."

She gazed up at him, her blue eyes glowing with desire. "So you do believe in it?"

"Since a golden haired woman with a cherub mouth came climbing up my apple tree and peeked at me through the leaves. It was a new sight for this mortal." His dark head lowered.

"You are a heavenly sight, *mon amour*," he whispered before his mouth closed over hers, giving her a taste of their glorious future.

* * * * *

Rancher Ramsey Westmoreland's temporary cook is way too attractive for his liking. Little does he know Chloe Burton came to his ranch with another agenda entirely....

That man across the street had to be, without a doubt, the most handsome man she'd ever seen.

Chloe Burton's pulse beat rhythmically as he stopped to talk to another man in front of a feed store. He was tall, dark and every inch of sexy—from his Stetson to the well-worn leather boots on his feet. And from the way his jeans and Western shirt fit his broad muscular shoulders, it was quite obvious he had everything it took to separate the men from the boys. The combination was enough to corrupt any woman's mind and had her weakening even from a distance. Her body felt flushed. It was hot. Unsettled.

Over the past year the only male who had gotten her time and attention had been the e-mail. That was simply pathetic, especially since now she was practically drooling simply at the sight of a man. Even his stance—both hands in his jeans pockets, legs braced apart, was a pose she would carry to her dreams.

And he was smiling, evidently enjoying the conversation being exchanged. He had dimples, incredibly sexy dimples in not one but both cheeks.

"What are you staring at, Clo?"

Chloe nearly jumped. She'd forgotten she had a lunch date. She glanced over the table at her best friend from college, Lucia Conyers.

"Take a look at that man across the street in the blue shirt, Lucia. Will he not be perfect for Denver's first issue of *Simply Irresistible* or what?" Chloe asked with so much excitement she almost couldn't stand it.

She was the owner of *Simply Irresistible*, a magazine for today's up-and-coming woman. Their once-a-year Irresistible Man cover, which highlighted a man the magazine felt deserved the honor, had increased sales enough for Chloe to open a Denver office.

When Lucia didn't say anything but kept staring, Chloe's smile widened. "Well?"

Lucia glanced across the booth at her. "Since you asked, I'll tell you what I see. One of the Westmorelands—Ramsey Westmoreland. And yes, he'd be perfect for the cover, but he won't do it."

Chloe raised a brow. "He'd get paid for his services, of course."

Lucia laughed and shook her head. "Getting paid won't be the issue, Clo—Ramsey is one of the wealthiest sheep ranchers in this part of Colorado. But everyone knows what a private person he is. Trust me—he won't do it."

Chloe couldn't help but smile. The man was the epitome of what she was looking for in a magazine cover and she was determined that whatever it took, he would be it.

"Umm, I don't like that look on your face, Chloe. I've seen it before and know exactly what it means."

She watched as Ramsey Westmoreland entered the store with a swagger that made her almost breathless. She *would* be seeing him again.

Look for Silhouette Desire's
HOT WESTMORELAND NIGHTS
by Brenda Jackson,
available March 9 wherever books are sold.

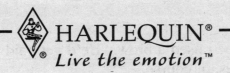

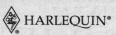

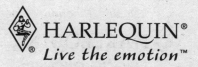

HARLEQUIN®
INTRIGUE®

BREATHTAKING ROMANTIC SUSPENSE

Shared dangers and passions lead to electrifying romance and heart-stopping suspense!

Every month, you'll meet six new heroes who are guaranteed to make your spine tingle and your pulse pound. With them you'll enter into the exciting world of Harlequin Intrigue—
where your life is on the line
and so is your heart!

THAT'S INTRIGUE—
ROMANTIC SUSPENSE
AT ITS BEST!

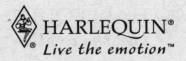

HARLEQUIN®
Live the emotion™

...there's more to the story!

Superromance.
A *big* satisfying read about unforgettable characters. Each month we offer *six* very different stories that range from family drama to adventure and mystery, from highly emotional stories to romantic comedies—and much more! Stories about people you'll believe in and care about. Stories too compelling to put down....

Our authors are among today's *best* romance writers. You'll find familiar names and talented newcomers. Many of them are award winners—and you'll see why!

If you want the biggest and best in romance fiction, you'll get it from Superromance!

Exciting, Emotional, Unexpected...

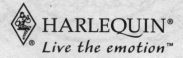

HARLEQUIN®
Live the emotion™

Harlequin® Historical
Historical Romantic Adventure!

Imagine a time of chivalrous knights and unconventional ladies, roguish rakes and impetuous heiresses, rugged cowboys and spirited frontierswomen— these rich and vivid tales will capture your imagination!

Harlequin Historical . . . they're too good to miss!